Make Mine a Gangsta

The Patton Brothers
Book 1

K.L. Hall

B. Love Publications

Make Mine a Gangsta Synopsis

It started with a proposition (*in a hotel bar of all places*).

The brooding drug lord. The beautiful damsel with jagged edges. You know the rest, right?

It's a page straight out of a hood fairy tale.

But our story is far from a classic romance.

Because Ahsan Patton isn't your typical gangsta.

He's the kind that'll order a hit then rearrange your guts to a slow jam.

So, tell me why I agreed to be his fake girlfriend again?

Now I'm sharing the same air with a man that oozes irresistible charm, money, and power.

The longer I'm in his presence, the quicker the lines blur between what's fact and fiction.

Our relationship? Faker than a three-dollar bill.

The way he makes me feel when he eats me like supper? Real AF.

There are rules to playing a couple. No outside dates. No talking about our arrangement to anyone. No falling in love.

Should be easy, right?

Until the minute I let my heart take the reins. Then all bets are off.

Ahsan Patton

2 *:30 A.M.*

The familiar jingle of my factory iPhone ringtone sounded off, jarring me from rest. I rolled over, first seeing the time displayed in white, neon lighting on the Echo Dot on my nightstand. Then, I looked at my phone. I swiped to accept the unknown number with a Las Vegas area code and put the phone to my ear.

"The fuck is this?" I growled into the receiver.

"You have a collect call from Las Vegas City Jail. Do you accept the charges?"

"What the fuck?" I grumbled as I rubbed the sleep out of my eyes and sat up in my king-sized bed. "I accept."

The operator connected the call, and seconds later, I heard my younger brother's familiar voice on the other end of the phone. "Yo, Ahsan. It's me, nigga. I need you to bail me out."

"Bail you out? Nigga, what the fuck happened?"

"It's Brandi, yo. You know how her ass is when she gets upset."

I sucked my teeth. "You let her ass call the cops on you?"

"Nah, nigga. I'm the one who called the fuckin' cops. She was swinging at me and yelling and shit. She turned into a whole Tasmanian devil on my black ass. They showed up, and then she started playing the victim, and I was the one who got arrested."

"The fuck they arrest you for? You hit her? You mark her ass up?"

He smacked his lips, just as annoyed with my questions as I was with his actions. "Nigga, no. You know I know better than that! I ain't do shit!"

"What they book you for, Amir?" I questioned with exasperation in my tone.

"I don't know, some bullshit disorderly conduct or domestic dispute or something. But I swear on Big Mama, I ain't put my hands on her. I was just trying to keep the fuckin' peace!" he explained.

I wagged my head. I knew Amir and Brandi were dramatic. They asses needed their own reality show. At least then, they'd get paid for acting as childish as they did. Amir was pushing thirty and still living life on the knife's edge. He thrived in that toxic shit. It was like his playground or something. It couldn't be me.

He was five years my junior and still sometimes acted as clueless as a newborn baby. If he kept fucking around with Brandi, he risked the heat coming down on him and me. We didn't need to mix and mingle with the Vegas PD when it wasn't necessary. If he was going to take my place in the game, he needed to start proving himself. But he was blood, and I loved him the most of anyone living. Overall, it all came down to loyalty.

"You comin' or what?" he queried, returning me to the present.

I cleared my throat before pulling the phone away to send a quick text. "I'm sending the lawyer to bail you out, and then I'ma deal with you later."

"The lawyer? Come on, nigga. I'm not trying to spend the rest of the night in here. Just come get me!"

I glanced at the time. I still had two and a half hours before my alarm went off. "I got a lot of shit to do today, and bailing your black ass out of jail ain't one of 'em, nigga. Sit and think about what you did until he gets there." I reprimanded him before ending the call.

I returned the phone to the nightstand and rolled over with a hard sigh. On my thirtieth birthday, I made a five-year plan. To date, I'd hit every goal I set for myself. With my thirty-fifth birthday just months away, the only thing I had left to do was go legit for real. To the outside world, I owned a trucking company with access to shipping routes across the U.S. To those needing to know, I was the head of a nefarious drug operation that spanned from Las Vegas to the Midwest, South, West, and East Coasts.

My seat was at the top of the Nevada food chain. I had wealth, street smarts, and impeccable style. I'd come a long way from being born addicted to crack cocaine and standing on street corners selling the shit. However, I'd made enough money to leave the illegal shit behind and was ready to hand over the reins to my brother, Amir. But his actions had shown me I probably needed to consider someone else for the role if he couldn't get his shit together.

LATER THAT MORNING, I MET MY COUSIN, KENDRICK "XL" Patton, at his barbershop to discuss business before it opened. Soon, the space would be filled with men gathering to debate over politics, trash talk about sports, and play rounds of chess and checkers. It would no longer be a safe space to discuss business. I sat at his station in his classic black barber chair while he gave me a quick edge up. I looked around at the framed black-and-white photos of iconic firsts, like the ribbon-cutting ceremony and snapshots of famous celebs who'd come through for a cut and some conversation. The sound of nineties and early 2000s R&B and hip-hop lulled in the background.

My cousin was one of the West's most skilled and experienced barbers. He was the only one I trusted with a pair of clippers and the only chair I'd ever sit in. He was a big boy who loved to cook almost as much as he loved getting niggas fresher than produce. He had a full, lumberjack-style beard that stretched from one ear to the other and a fresh, low-wave fade. His dark chocolate brown eyes matched his cocoa complexion. His freshly lined goatee sat under his wide-set nose and wrapped around his lips. Around his neck was his favorite gold Cuban link chain with a diamond-encrusted skull hanging from it. He'd purchased it with the first real money we got coming up and never took it off. He called it his good luck charm.

XL was my mother's nephew. Our grandmother, Big Mama, raised him alongside Amir and me because both of our mothers were strung out on crack cocaine and heroin and eventually died on the needle. She was our mother, and the streets were our father. We went from pre-teen corner boys to the top of the drug food chain. His barbershop was just one of the places we washed our money through. Aside from being my cousin and my barber, he was my confidante.

"So, wassup, nigga?" he asked over the buzzing sound of the clippers.

I swiped my hand down my beard. "It's Amir, man. Nigga got arrested earlier this morning."

His bushy eyebrows heightened. "Arrested? For what?"

"Fucking around with that crazy broad, Brandi. He called the cops on her, and his ass ended up being the one who got arrested and called me at two in the morning to bail him out. I hit the lawyer to get him."

He shook his head. "I swear that nigga loves the drama."

"Exactly! It doesn't matter how much I instill common sense in him. He don't fuckin' listen," I griped.

"You know how the game goes. Nigga will learn the lesson when it's his time to, and he'll grow when he's supposed to grow."

I sucked my teeth, brushing off his uplifting outlook on that shit. "At this point, he should know we don't need the unnecessary attention. We been doing this since Kermit was a tadpole."

He nodded in agreement. "That's for damn sure. And ain't caught a case or a bullet yet."

I chuckled. "Look at Big Mama's prayers, which are still working wonders after all these years."

He joined me in a laugh. "Hallelujah and amen, nigga."

"But I'm ready for a change, a big one."

I caught his eyes staring at my reflection in the large mirror. "Like what?" he inquired.

"You know I'm turning thirty-five in a few months. I'm ready to move into the final phase of my plan."

"You and this plan of yours, nigga. What's up now?"

"I thought I was ready to hand everything over to Amir, but now I'm having second thoughts behind that shit."

"Second thoughts? Why? He's family."

"Family fucks up too."

"Yeah, but just because he had one fuck up don't mean he'll have another one."

"With that bitch Brandi around, there will always be another one," I forewarned.

Before he could respond, my phone buzzed in my lap. I looked down at the screen to see my office number. "Hello?" I answered.

"Hey. What time will you be at the office? One of the drivers called. There's an issue with the Houston shipment," my assistant, Jules, announced.

"What kind of issue?"

"Trucks are late, and the phones are starting to ring nonstop," she informed me.

Jules was my assistant and the *only* woman I kept around me consistently. She was the only woman I kept around me, period. Yet, I still didn't trust her enough to let her in on my underground business. I kept separate files and financial books to hide the truth regarding my illegal dealings. For the last few years, I'd sworn off women for all intents and purposes outside of fucking, to focus solely on my money moves and my five-year plan.

My outlook on women, and relationships in general, was laced with doubt. I always feared a bitch's underlying motives, acting like shit was sweet in the beginning just to take my money in the end. I'd never let a bitch trick me off the street. My relationship with Jules was different. It was strictly business. She'd worked for me for the past four years and knew my schedule better than her own. I trusted her to do her job, and she did it well.

"Tell them they'll get what they need, and the shipment is still coming. I'll be there soon," I responded before ending the call.

XL and I traded glances in the mirror. "Everything good?"

"There's been a change in the weather. The snow ain't falling in Houston tonight," I informed him, speaking in code. "I gotta go."

"You want me to check in on Amir for you?" he offered while unhooking the smock around my neck.

"Yeah. Knock some sense into his dumb ass for me when you see 'em."

XL belted out a hearty chuckle. "I got you."

Sienna Bennett

The mid-afternoon sun sifted through the blinds inside the living room of the small one-bedroom apartment I shared with my cousin Zyon casting tiger-striped shadows across the threadbare carpet. She and I sat on the second-hand leather couch we'd rescued from the curb, staring at the pile of bills on the coffee table. I cut my eyes at her, my expression a mix of irritation and worry as I pulled my curly hair up into a high bun.

"Zy, the rent is weeks overdue, and Mr. Franklin is already on our ass. He ain't gon' wait forever. Please tell me you got your half this month."

She impatiently tapped her phone screen. "Fuck Mr. Franklin."

I sucked my teeth. "Stop playin', Zy. I'm serious! We gotta figure this money shit out before both our asses be out on the street selling ass on the Strip!"

She leaned against the couch and sighed. "Shit has been slow. What do you want me to do?"

My eyes narrowed. "I want you to be an adult and help me pay these fucking bills! How are we supposed to come up with the money?"

"Maybe we can ask my mama for help. She's always preaching that shit about family needing to stick together more now than ever."

I swung my head in a no. "Hell no, Zy. You know how Aunt Sheila is. She'll lecture us about being adults and the responsibilities that come with it. Then, run and tell my mama then everyone and their mama at church! We don't need people in our business."

She snickered. "Guess we can't all spend our extra coins on washable paint and colored pencils like you."

I rolled my eyes at her weak-ass joke. We loved each other but disagreed on many things, especially money and education. My eyes darted to the stack of unfinished art pieces leaning against my easel near the window. I dropped out of college a year and a half ago after failing to balance the late nights working at the strip club and my early classes. My goal was to return as soon as I'd paid off my debt and saved up enough money to pay for four full years of tuition. The irony of it was when I had the time for school and focusing on my craft, I couldn't afford it, and when I was able to start putting money aside so I could finally fucking pay my way, there never seemed to be enough hours in the day.

Zyon's cocoa-brown eyes looked around our tiny shared space, for which we paid $1,500 monthly to rent. I studied how she wrinkled her slim, pierced nose or flipped her burgundy beach waves over her shoulder while batting the fresh set of faux mink lashes. Zyon shifted her weight from one leg to the other, poking out her hip and accentuating her slim-thick build.

"We could sell some shit. Maybe the TV?" she suggested.

Our apartment walls were a warm beige and adorned with a few framed motivational quotes. A faux succulent plant was on the coffee table, and fairy lights zigzagged across the ceiling. The air conditioning unit in the window hummed, cooling the intimate space. The air around us smelled of incense—sandalwood and lavender— mingling with the aroma of the seasoned chicken wings Zy had fried a few hours earlier.

Zy's blue and green lava lamp sat on the windowsill, its blue and green blobs of color slowly moving around the glass. Outside the window was a view of the outlying mountains and iconic Vegas Strip looming in the distance, its neon lights flickering twenty-four-seven.

I frowned. "Say that pays for rent, then what about groceries? We can't live on Ramen and Chef Boyardee forever."

Before she responded, my phone buzzed with a text. A groan escaped my lips as soon as I checked it. "Mr. Franklin just sent another text. Fuck, man. He says we've got three days to pay this month and at least half of the back rent from the last month, or we're facing eviction."

"Again, *fuck* Mr. Franklin," she repeated with just as much disdain in her tone as she had previously.

"No, fuck you, Zy! I'm not roaming the fucking Strip for bait like I did last month for your ass! Ballers don't walk the Strip. They own the hotels and restaurants on the Strip. You see the difference? I'll just be wasting my time!"

Zyon crossed her milk chocolate arms. "Looks like we need a miracle, Sienna."

I scoffed. "That, or a winning fucking lottery ticket."

She chuckled. "Yeah, well, until that shit happens, let's put our heads together. Maybe we both can pick up extra shifts at the club or take one of those private parties Sparkle and Diamond are always running their traps about."

I was twenty-four years old and had been stripping since two weeks after my twenty-first birthday. Every month, I paid my half of the bills and sent money back home to my mama when I could afford to help her out. On top of that, I was on a payment plan to pay off my outstanding tuition so that I would be back in good standing when I reapplied for the arts program, and I was still trying to save money for my return.

Although I was the definition of a starving artist, I wanted to be taken seriously in the art industry. In a perfect world, I'd be living somewhere with the dopest, unhindered view of the city or some large, uninterrupted body of water with my easel and a blank canvas, ready to paint whatever the fuck I was inspired to. But a girl could dream, right? Stripper money was decent, but it hadn't gotten me any closer to becoming a millionaire or living the lifestyle I'd always dreamed of.

I shrugged my shoulders, snapping out of my thoughts that had me anywhere but where I was. "I don't know. We may have to start doing them if it's going to continue to be this hard to make ends meet."

Zyon also stripped at the same club and moonlighted as a bartender at different bars on the Strip. But, it was the middle of the summer, which was typically Vegas's off-season due to the scorching heat, which meant money wasn't flowing like a river.

"I don't know why you're trippin'. I'm sure we'll be straight. It'll all shake out like it always does."

I folded my arms across my chest. "And what about last month's half or the half before that? Because we still waiting on that shit to 'shake out,'" I said in air quotes, mocking her.

"Chill, Sienna. You over here talking about my mama preaching, and your ass right there in the pulpit with her!"

"I don't see why you're not taking this more seriously, especially when you don't have your half. Do you need to read the text yourself? Mr. Franklin's serious, Zy. If we can't come up with the money, that's our asses!"

"You working at the club tonight?" she asked, changing the subject.

"Yeah."

"Guess you better shake that ass real hard tonight then, huh?" she cackled with a sarcastic smirk.

I smacked my lips. "Fuck you, Zy! Keep fucking around, and you gon' have to really fuck Mr. Franklin instead of just saying it!" I prewarned her before storming down the hall.

Ahsan

I stepped inside Big Mama's hospital room in the ICU. The faint scent of my cologne mingled with the smell of antiseptic in the air as I tore my eyes over to the bed in the center of the cold, scuffed floor. The metal rails were up, and her pillow looked plump underneath her. I wanted her to be comfortable, even if she never lifted her head again. Big Mama lay on the bed, her frail body hidden underneath a white hospital blanket. Tubes snaked from the wall to her bedside, connecting her to the beeping monitors and the ventilator—the life-saving machine that kept her breathing and still a part of the land of the living.

Mounted on the pale wall was a small flat-screen television playing reruns of *Murder She Wrote*. It was Big Mama's favorite show. She loved to hate Angela Lansbury's old, white ass. As always, I walked over to the bed and kissed her forehead before sitting in the worn armchair by the window. The view from her window was framed by faded blue curtains that overlooked the hospital garden in the center of the courtyard. Although she hadn't opened her eyes since her stroke, it brought me joy knowing beauty awaited her right outside her window.

I glanced back over at the bed. On her bedside table was a family photo of Big Mama, my brother, our cousin, XL, and me on her sixty-fifth birthday a few years back. Big Mama smiled, her eyes crinkled at the corners with genuine laughter, surrounded by "her boys," as she called us. I'd been overprotective of her health ever since she had a heart attack five years ago. Just when everything started to get on track, she fucked around and had a severe stroke. Since she'd been hospitalized, she'd been under around-the-clock monitoring and in a coma for almost two weeks, with no signs of waking up.

At some point, everyone had to deal with the pain of losing someone they loved. Death was an inevitable part of life. Even still, I refused to talk about the possibility of a world where she didn't exist anymore, even if I knew it was likely to happen sooner than later. I shifted my attention toward the door when I heard a knock. Dr. Baker, a middle-aged Caucasian woman with brown hair and kind eyes, entered the room. She wore a white lab coat that looked too big for her petite frame. Her footsteps crossed the vinyl floor as she approached me.

"Nice to see you again, Mr. Patton." She greeted me in a gentle voice. "Will your brother or cousin be stopping by?"

"They're downstairs in the waiting area, waiting for me to come down and tag one of 'em in. Wassup? Is it important? I can call and tell them to come up."

The hospital limited ICU visitors to two at a time, so we all took turns coming up one by one when all three of us were here to see her.

"You're her power of attorney, right?"

I dipped my chin. "Yeah."

"Well, I'd like to speak directly to you if that's okay."

"Sure."

"Thank you, Mr. Patton. I've thoroughly reviewed your grand-mother's case. I wish I had better news for you. But unfortunately, her condition hasn't improved. She remains in a deep coma after her stroke, and according to her latest scans, there is minimal brain activity, which means there's little to no chance she'll wake up."

My throat tightened as I nodded, unable to find my words. Facing the possibility of losing Big Mama was something I wasn't ready to do.

Dr. Baker continued. "Given the circumstances, we need to discuss next steps. I know what I'm about to say will be difficult to hear, but it may be time to consider stopping life-sustaining treatment," she said firmly.

"What are her chances of recovery if you take her off life support?"

"I know this is a tough decision to make, Mr. Patton. But, speaking as her medical professional, your grandmother's quality of life is declining, and prolonging her pain may not be in her best interest or your family's."

Tears welled up in my eyes the minute I glanced at Big Mama. Her chest rose and fell rhythmically with the assistance of the ventilator. Memories flooded my mind—the stories she'd told us about our mothers when they were our ages to keep a pleasant memory of them alive, the warmth of her embrace after a hard night hugging the block, the smell of her iconic baked mac and cheese.

"So this is your final recommendation?" I finally managed to ask while swiping my hand down my beard.

The doctor stood at the foot of Big Mama's bed, her gaze steady as she sighed. "I recommend you, your brother, and your cousin spend as much time with her as you want and prepare to say your goodbyes. We'll give it another week, but if there's no improvement, we'll have to strongly consider withdrawing life support."

I nodded, my heart heavy as a ton of gold bricks. I stood up and walked over to Big Mama's bedside. I reached for her hand, her mocha brown skin dry and fragile. "Thank you, Dr. Baker," I whispered. "I'll make sure to do what's best for her."

She patted my shoulder. "I'll have the nurse bring in some

emotional support pamphlets. Connecting with others who are grieving can really help families cope during difficult times."

As the doctor exited the room, I remained by Big Mama's side, the weight of the unsettling decision settling on my shoulders. Life support was the only thing that helped her stay alive. Pulling the plug wasn't something I'd ever considered doing. Time stood still as if suspended somewhere between life and death. Because, in reality, it was.

I STEPPED OUT OF THE ELEVATOR ON THE FIRST FLOOR AND trekked down the long, maze-like hallway to the waiting area where Amir and XL were.

XL locked eyes with me as I approached them. "Wassup?"

I dapped him up. "Yo. The doctor came while I was up there," I informed them.

"Yeah?" Amir asked. "What she say? Any changes in Big Mama's condition?"

"Any news on when she'll wake up?" XL added.

I swung my head in a no. "Nah."

XL studied the unease in my expression. "You wanna step outside?"

I nodded, and the three of us switched locations from the hospital waiting area to the parking lot. Instantly, I felt the sun's scorching rays paint my milk chocolate skin with its light.

"Now, what did the doctor say?" XL asked.

"She said it's not looking good for Big Mama. Something about her last scans not showing any brain activity. She thinks we should consider..."

"What? Consider what?" Amir asked, eager for the answer.

My chest deflated with a long sigh. "She wants us to consider taking Big Mama off life support."

Amir huffed as his brows shot up toward his crisp hairline. "The fuck? I don't give a fuck what that doctor says! I'm not pulling the plug on Big Mama!"

"I hear what you're saying, but I don't want her to be a fuckin' vegetable layin' up there either just because we're too pussy to say goodbye!" I argued back.

She had life insurance and a will, but we all still refused to accept her terminal diagnosis. It was as if we'd all been reduced from grown-ass men to scared little boys.

"Can we get a second opinion?" XL inquired, being the voice of reason.

"It's too late for that. She's been in a coma for weeks now."

"People wake up from comas after being asleep for years! Why the fuck she want us to pull the plug so soon? Because we black?"

"It's not like we can't afford to move her somewhere else and give her the same around-the-clock care she gets here," XL suggested.

Amir's hands shot toward the sky. "See! There's another idea! I like that better than puttin' Big Mama in the ground."

I grunted, knowing we wouldn't all come to an easy agreement on Big Mama's care. But at the end of the day, I was her power of attorney, and I had the final say.

I cleared my throat. "We ain't gon' come to an agreement today, and ain't nobody making any permanent decisions right now. Aside from Big Mama, we need to talk about the next re-up. I plan for this to be my biggest and last one from our connect down in Mexico."

"When's the next shipment due?" Amir quizzed.

"Next Thursday. Then I'm out of the game for good."

"You sure you ready to hand all this shit over?"

"Yeah, nigga," XL added. "You ready to swap out them joggers for a tailor-made suit?"

"I'm ready. Everything is going according to my plan."

Amir sucked his teeth. "Aw, hell. There he go with this plan shit again."

XL chuckled. "You ain't gotta explain it to us, boss. We know you got all your moves already calculated up there in that big-ass brain of yours," he stated before tapping his temple with his index and middle fingers.

I brushed off their comments. When I turned thirty, I completely changed my mindset and decided to create a five-year plan to get out of the game and stick to that shit like glue. I hadn't waivered yet and was months away from seeing year thirty-five. By this point, they knew my intentions as well as I did. I wanted to make money in my sleep from more than just drug trafficking. I started making smart investments and strategic partnerships with businessmen who didn't make their deals in the streets like we were used to.

Growing up, I was the only one out of our trio who enjoyed at least some parts of school—only math, business, and chemistry. Fuck all that other shit. My math skills helped me keep my paper right on the streets. You had to be quick with the numbers in your head if you didn't wanna get fucked over. My interest in business was self-explanatory. And chemistry? I enjoyed the science behind knowing how to make a body disappear without a trace. Never knew when something like that would come in handy one day.

Sienna

I stepped into the pulsating heart of the strip club I worked at called Dazzle. The electric blue and hot pink neon hues flooded my sight as the thumping beat of rap music reverberated through the space, damn near shaking the walls. The air crackled with the smell of fresh one-dollar bills and waxed pussy. The bar stretched along the wall to my right. All female bartenders in leather hot pants and bustiers mixed strong drinks, some glowing to match the bright lights. The Dazzler cocktail was our most popular drink. It was a strong-ass pink martini rimmed with neon sugar. It kept us lifted and feeling good on that stage.

At the center of the room stood the stage, my playground. It was a glass platform surrounded by mirrors. It reflected the crowd, multiplying bodies and colors, especially if a bitch was buzzed. A dancer named Vixen was on stage. She was a baddie, moving her sweat-slicked and euphoric body to the beat. Other dancers, clad in tassels and tips, popped their asses in the crowd while stuffing their G-strings with as many dirty dollars as possible before the money well dried up for the night. DJ VIP commanded the booth to the left of the stage, keeping everybody in the club with their hands raised, lost in the rhythm and the sea of ass. Then, there was the VIP area, a raised section behind black velvet ropes. That was where the glitterati gathered, meaning ballers and celebs.

I pushed open the heavy velvet curtains to the dressing room, letting the world fade behind me. Chris, the bouncer, nodded as I stepped inside. The paint-chipped walls were covered with graffiti, glowing under the UV lights. I walked over to my vanity and sat down. My long, Brazilian body wave wig was parted down the middle, framing my slim face. I put a bit of mascara on the end of my false lashes to accentuate them a little more and put diamond sparkles in the corners of my eyes to give my soft, glam makeup the final pop. Next, I'd filled in my brows and was about to apply some eyeliner when I saw Sparkle and Diamond walk in. My conversation with Zyon resurfaced in my head about their private parties. So, I figured I'd go over to them and inquire about their next gig and let them know Zyon and I were trying to be down like Brandy.

I strolled around to their side-by-side stations and caught Diamond's honey-brown eyes staring back at me through her reflection. She wore a blunt cut, bleach blonde bob wig, and a red leather two-piece lingerie set. Her perky breasts sat high on her chest, and her makeup was flawless—from her dramatic mink lashes to the accentuation of her brow bone and over-glossed lips. Sparkle, on the other hand, had bundles of raw Brazilian hair flowing down her back to the crack of her ass. She was a chocolate chick and thick as hell. Her waist was just as tiny as Diamond's, but what she lacked in cup size, she made up for in ass. All the niggas loved to see Sparkle coming but loved watching her leave even more.

"Wassup? Y'all got a minute?"

"What you want, Bella?" Diamond queried, calling me by my stage name.

"You know those private parties you two are always talking about?"

"What about them?" Sparkle quizzed.

My chest deflated with a drawn-out sigh. "Well, me and my

cousin wanna be down on your next one. You got one coming up soon?"

They traded glances before Diamond spoke up. "How can I put this? We've scaled our pussy popping game to the next level."

Sparkle nodded in agreement. "Exactly. We only deal with high-level clientele now."

"High-level clientele? Like the niggas that be in VIP?"

Sparkle swung her head in a no while turning up her nose. "Ew, bitch. Think bigger."

"And with way longer money," Diamond added.

"We know where all the paid ballers be at in the city at any given time. I'm talking tech tycoons and CEOs, to politicians and ball players."

I cocked my head to the side, leery of getting too excited too quickly. "If y'all got all this access and clout now, why the fuck you still shaking ass at this hole in the wall?"

Diamond scoffed. "Gotta make all this extra money look legit to the IRS somehow. And last I checked, they weren't auditing strippers. But you watch; we won't be here for long. I'ma either get me a ring or have me a baby by one of these rich ass niggas."

"Guess you got it all figured out, huh?"

Sparkle nodded. "Yup."

Diamond agreed. "Sho do."

I had a laundry list of reservations about why I didn't want to take things to the next step, but I had a million and one bills that said otherwise. "I wanna be down. Put me on. How do I get on?"

"Chill, eager beaver. What's the urgency?" Diamond asked.

"I got more bills than I got money. Plus, shit is drying up out there. But you already knew that, or else you wouldn't be into these extracurricular activities."

"The girl has a point there," Sparkle added.

"What all do you have to do with these high-level clientele niggas?"

Diamond shrugged her lean shoulders. "Whatever they pay us to do."

I shrugged with a curious look on my face. "And you're okay with... y'know, sellin' your pussy for money?"

Sparkle scoffed. "It's Vegas, baby. The shit is legal. If you got a bug up your ass about it, why the fuck you over here asking so many questions, Inspector Gadget?"

"I'm not judging. I just wanna know how you feel about it."

"I don't feel. I don't get paid to do that shit. And even if I did, I wouldn't. Here, I get paid to dance. There, I get paid to fuck. That's it, that's all."

"So, basically, you're saying, be a robot."

"Be whatever you gotta be until you're filthy fucking rich. Escorting is a job like any other," Sparkle explained.

I nodded. She had a wild way of putting shit, but I understood where she was coming from. She just didn't know how real my struggle was. I hadn't spoken to Zyon since our fallout about the rent, and I'd been ducking our landlord like the plague. We'd all gotten to the point where we told ourselves it was okay to go a little further, then a little further, until there were no more limits to what we wouldn't do for money.

"Thanks for the information."

I walked back to my vanity with a lot to think about, one being how I got to where I was in life. I was only twenty-four and felt like I'd already lived such a hard life. Zyon and I moved out to Vegas from Miami when we were eighteen. Our families were still back in Florida. She kept in contact with her mama and brother. My mother and I hadn't had a good relationship in almost five years, because she disagreed with the life I'd chosen to live. Yet, I never heard one complaint about my devil dollars whenever I wired her money to help keep a roof over her head. I was ready to be in my soft girl era, be spoiled and catered to, even if I had to fuck for money to do it.

Truth be told, I didn't fuck with niggas because they never knew how to act long-term. Ever. Games were for kids, and I was too damn grown to be playing around. I'd only been in one serious relationship, which didn't end with a happily ever after. Far from it. After that, I vowed I'd never trust another nigga with my heart again. It was better to keep it on ice.

I knew how to make a nigga feel like he was the only one I had my eye on in the whole club. I learned how to move my hips in a way that made a nigga think my pussy was for him and him only. I'd been running games on niggas like Nintendo for years, but nothing to this extreme. Could I fake orgasms and interest for money?

It's only for a little while. Once I can pay for four years of tuition, I can walk away from all this shit for good. I had a little less than $5,000 left of tuition to pay off, and with the money I'd saved up for the past nine months, I only had $1,200 left. I'd been dipping into my school savings to cover the bills and pay for groceries, but I refused to dip into it again, all because my broke-ass cousin couldn't make the rent. I loved Zyon. I swear I did. But living with her was like being a crab in a barrel. She worked double-time to bring me back down whenever I tried to get out.

"*Fuck,*" I mumbled before walking back over to their vanities. "I'm in. What I gotta do?"

Diamond smirked. "Say less. Put your number in my phone. When we have something, I'll hit your line."

"Remember, it's hunting season," Sparkle interjected. "You don't work, you don't eat. So be ready when we call."

I dipped my chin. "I will be."

Ahsan

I sat behind my mahogany desk, staring at the view outside my office window. My trucking business flourished over the last eight years, making me a prominent figure in the city. My invitation to the upcoming annual business gala was a testament to my success. I turned my attention toward the door when I heard a knock.

"Got a minute?" Jules asked, standing in the doorframe. "I wanted to go over your latest schedule updates with you."

"Yeah. Come in."

She stepped inside and closed the door behind her. She carried a black tablet in one hand and her coffee cup in the other as her heels clicked against the hardwood floor. She was in her late twenties and stood at about five feet five. Her skin was a rich shade of mocha, and her expressive brown eyes were dark and knowing, seemingly never missing a beat. Her hair was styled in a long, bone-straight sew-in with layers framing her slim face. She wore a tailored navy-blue pantsuit that emphasized her slender figure. A gold Cartier bracelet adorned her right wrist, a subtle touch of high class.

Jules adjusted her square-framed glasses she wore more for fashion than for vision before taking her seat on the edge of my desk.

She scrolled through the digital schedule. "Okay, so we've got the Annual Las Vegas Business Leaders Gala at the Grand Mirage Hotel next weekend," she said. "I'm talking city officials, business moguls, and top execs—the whole shebang. It's going to be a fucking networking gold mine."

I leaned back in my chair, considering. "I need face time with Mayor Dinkins to discuss my business and land development proposal."

The business proposal was at the epicenter of my five-year plan. Not only did I want to expand my logistics network deeper into Texas, but it also included a comprehensive plan for land development to build affordable housing and retail space for black-owned businesses in Vegas. By partnering with the city, I hoped to create a win-win arrangement: improved quality of living for the community, a financial boost in the economy, and increased business opportunities for my trucking company in Nevada and beyond. It was my chance to prove myself in a new arena.

"This gala is your chance to do that. There's just one last thing."

"What?"

"You need a date, Ahsan."

I arched a questioning brow. "A date? For what?"

She leaned in, her expression serious. "No offense, but you'll stand out like a sore thumb. You'll be a successful African American entrepreneur in a sea of tuxes and gowns with no date on your arm. We need you to blend in and make connections. And what better way than with a charming companion? Besides, the mayor is a family man. I'm willing to bet my salary his wife will be there."

"Shit." I hissed. "I didn't think about that."

She pulled her glasses away from her face before sweeping a lock of her hair behind her ear. "I could find someone for you, or I guess I could go with you since it's such short notice."

I chuckled. "You volunteering, Jules?"

She grinned. "I mean, I could if you needed me to, but—"

"No. You're right. Find me someone for the night and get me the event info."

She swallowed hard with a nod before putting her glasses back on. "It's already on your calendar, and sure. I'll handle it."

I knew she was sharp-witted, and I trusted her judgment. "Bet. Thank you. I don't know what I'd do without you."

Jules tapped her tablet. "I'm here to make your life easier, Ahsan. Consider it done."

She set off on her mission. The thought crossed my mind, wondering if she'd choose a polished executive, a model, or someone completely unexpected. Either way, with a gorgeous date by my side, I was ready to step into the spotlight and make my mark on the city that reveled in sin.

LATER THAT EVENING, I STEPPED INTO MY CONDO, THE CITY'S bright glow shining through my floor-to-ceiling windows. I kicked off my shoes and sank into the welcoming plush carpet. My spacious place was lavish, with polished marble floors stretching across the open floorplan. A sleek, white Italian leather sofa faced the large flat-screen TV I rarely turned on. The eggshell-painted walls were embellished with abstract art by black artists, and the untouched kitchen gleamed with spotless stainless steel appliances and granite countertops.

My balcony beckoned to me, a private oasis above the city's chaos. I stepped out, the dry desert night air wrapping around me. The glass railing offered an unobstructed view of the Strip, from the timed dance routines of the Bellagio fountains to the glowing replica of the Eiffel Tower. I opened my humidor and pulled out a pre-rolled blunt amongst my Cuban cigars. I flicked my lighter and lit the blunt, watching the thick smoke curl like ribbon.

And there, in the deafening silence, I felt the vast emptiness. Sin City buzzed beneath me, but I was secluded and untouchable. I'd climbed to the top of the food chain, but the peak was lonely. Before then, I never doubted my decision to trade in relationships and pillow talk for power and success. But I started to feel differently as I leaned against the railing and puffed my blunt while staring at the bright lights. With Big Mama's declining health lingering on my mind and the business gala on the horizon, it felt like the walls were closing in.

As the blunt burned down, I wondered for the first time what it would be like to have a non-transactional connection with a woman. Bitches always wanted something. Sometimes, I didn't mind spending bands on a female just for the hell of it, but it wasn't a recurring thing. I enjoyed my space, but it would've been dope to come home to a home-cooked meal and a back rub after a hard day. I needed something or someone to bridge the gap between success and seclusion.

Sienna

ne week later.

THE TV EMITTED A BRIGHT GLOW AS THE TALKING HEADS ON the screen mumbled in the background. I sat on the couch, attention zoned in on my phone. I hadn't heard from Diamond or Sparkle but had been sure to put Zyon on with the information too. Looking up from my phone, I heard Zyon burst through the front door and slam it behind her. I twisted my neck to see her holding a stack of mail and panting heavily as if she'd been running from the police.

"What the hell is wrong with you?"

She rested her back against the door before turning around to look through the peephole and whispering her response. "It was Mr. Franklin. I saw his ass down the hall at Apartment F when I got off the elevator. I ran in here so damn fast. I hope his ass didn't see me!"

I huffed, feeling the pang of resentment in my chest. "So, I take it this means you *still* don't have your half of the rent money?"

Zyon twisted her lips to the side as she trotted over to me. "Before we get to all that, I've got a lot of good and a little bad news. Which one do you want first?"

I raised a suspicious brow. "Bad news."

She leaned against the back of the couch. "Okay, brace yourself. You got a letter in the mail from D."

My heart galloped in my chest. "What?" My brows downturned, and my nose wrinkled as if I'd gotten a whiff of something foul. "How the fuck does he even know where I live?"

"It looks like it got forwarded here after going to your old address," she explained, studying the envelope.

Her revelation made my breaths ease back into a normal flow. "No. Throw it away. I don't want to see it."

"You sure?"

"Positive."

She nodded. "Fair enough. But you know he's like a brother to me. You're gonna have to deal with it eventually."

"Like a brother? I'm your blood, remember? That trumps fake siblings any day of the week," I snapped.

She didn't know how bad she'd triggered me. Demario had already been weighing heavy on my mind for the past few days. It was nearing the fifth anniversary of his imprisonment.

He'd served five years on a fifteen-year bid. Some years back, he and his boys got wrapped up with a shady group of niggas running an underground drug ring. D was twenty-three and a natural-born hustler, so he was always ready to hit a quick lick for some easy money. After his boys robbed a drug dealer named Chi, he agreed to transport a large shipment of narcotics across state lines with no questions asked.

Unfortunately, the police pulled him over, and he was caught red-handed with two kilos of coke and Chi's body in the trunk. He had a speedy trial and received a lengthy sentence for drug trafficking and kidnapping. Luckily, Chi wasn't found dead in that trunk, or he probably would've been charged with murder and sentenced to the needle.

I was eighteen when we locked eyes for the first time and nineteen when he went in. Initially, I didn't know his prison sentence would cast such a dark shadow over our relationship. I was young and in love. I didn't care that we hadn't been together a heartbeat longer than a year. All I cared about was supporting *my man, my man, my man.* I clung to him, believing I was his ride or die and that our love could conquer all. In the beginning, I visited him faithfully every month and wrote letters, pouring my heart out about what I envisioned our future being like beyond his prison walls.

But as the months turned into years, the tension grew thicker. His trust in me eroded, replaced by resentment and anger when he found out I was stripping to make ends meet. I felt torn between staying loyal to him and my own survival. I knew I loved him, but I also knew it was time to choose myself, which meant letting him go. So, I distanced myself from him, leaving myself heartbroken and in a sour mood for months before I found the courage to end things officially. All I wanted to do was move forward with my life. But with his unexpected letter in the mail, it was almost like he was forcing me to confront our past once again, and I wanted no parts.

"You ready for the good news now?" Zy queried, drawing me out of the rabbit hole I'd gone down inside my mind.

I huffed. "Anything is better than what the fuck you just said, so yeah. I'm ready."

"Remember that art gallery you submitted your paintings to last month?"

"Yeah. I never heard back. What about it?"

"They accepted your work!" she exclaimed, waving the letter in front of my face. "Your *Soul Ties* series will be exhibited next month. Sienna, this is fucking major! I know I make fun of you about your art and shit, but this is huge!"

My eyes doubled in size. "Are you fucking serious? Oh my God!" I shouted.

My face lit up as I jumped up from the couch and snatched the letter from Zyon's hands, momentarily forgetting about Demario and the fact that her nosy ass had opened my mail.

My eyes scanned the paper from left to right as the words danced off my tongue. "Dear Ms. Bennett, thank you for your recent submission to our art gallery. Your captivating pieces left a lasting mark on our selection committee. I am pleased to inform you that your *Soul Ties* series has been selected for next month's exhibition at the Gallery at Forestbrook. The 'Visions of Emotions' exhibition will showcase local talent across Nevada and celebrate their creativity. Your presence is requested at the gallery at six o'clock on the evening of Saturday, August twenty-fourth, for the grand reveal. Congratulations! Sincerely, Nia Sinclair, Curator, Gallery at Forestbrook."

My hand trembled as I clutched the letter to my chest, feeling the weight of my validation. The art gallery's upcoming exhibition was the sign I'd been needing. I'd been praying for a fresh start. I couldn't wait to see my vibrant paintings decorating the gallery walls. It was the first big step in the right direction for my art career, and I'd done it without an art degree.

"Congrats, cuzzo!" Zy said, reaching out to set the mail on the coffee table before hugging me.

I glanced at the coffee table, where the stack of mail sat with Demario's unopened letter on the top of the pile. My chest deflated with a sigh as I pried away from Zy's grasp. "Listen, about the rent. I hate to—"

"Wait! I told you there was a lot of good news."

"There's more?" I asked, arching a curious brow.

"Yeah. I talked to Sparkle."

"Really? What did she say? Because I haven't heard from her or Diamond since I told them we wanted to be down."

"Girl, all our money problems are about to be finito!"

"What do you mean?"

"Sparkle told me about this big ass business gala this weekend. It's some high-end event where all the big-time moneymakers will be.

Let her tell it, you can't even get in if you don't have a net worth of at least six figures."

"And they're going to that?" I quizzed.

She nodded quickly. "Yup, and so are we!"

"We are?"

"Hell yeah! I'm talking about a sea full of potentially eligible ballers, bitch. We need to go and find some connections, if you know what I mean."

I tore my eyes down to the floor. "I don't know."

"Annndddd, Sparkle's got ballers on her roster with house accounts with couture designers. She can get us some bomb-ass dresses! That way, we'll look the part."

"And then what?"

"Easy. We divide and conquer. We sit alone in the bar or lobby and let them come to us. As good as we'll look, we'll have niggas of all colors and creeds eating out the palms of our hands by the end of the night! It'll be just like working at the club."

I smirked while cocking my head to the side. "You got it all figured out, huh?"

Zy cheesed. "You just make sure you beat that pretty face of yours to perfection this Saturday, cousin. We gotta get this money!"

Ahsan

The night of the gala rolled around quicker than expected. I hadn't anticipated sitting behind the wheel of my sleek black sedan, frustrated as fuck and looking as good as I did. I'd slid through the shop earlier in the day and got a fresh cut from XL. That, coupled with my tailored, black tuxedo and the designer loafers on my feet that cost more than someone's rent, my swag was on a trillion. A grunt escaped my lips as I surveyed the chaos outside my windshield. The Las Vegas Strip, usually a glittering path of blinking neon lights, had transformed into a maze of traffic detours and flashing road signs. I glanced at the dashboard clock. The gala, the one that could elevate my entire fucking career, continued to slip away minute by minute. With no charging cord to revive it, my cell lay lifeless in the cup holder. The battery was drained, just like my chances of arriving on fucking time.

"Fuck," I grumbled.

I gripped the steering wheel, frustration bubbling up inside me. I needed a blunt to ease my nerves. The GPS on my dash rerouted me for the third time, leading me deeper into the maze of blocked streets. As the minutes passed, I imagined the business deals being made inside the grand ballroom amongst the city's power players. I pictured myself making the perfect pitch to the mayor and shaking hands to seal the deal. But my reality was a traffic jam with horns blaring and bumper-to-bumper traffic. Desperation fueled me, and for a second, I considered abandoning my car and sprinting toward the hotel. But I remained behind the wheel.

Jules had arranged for my date to meet me at the hotel. I was running so behind I was grateful I hadn't agreed to pick her up as well. For a second, I wondered if God really had a sense of humor. Maybe being in the gridlock of Las Vegas was exactly where I was supposed to be. I took a deep breath, focusing solely on the shit within my control. I was already over an hour late, and there was nothing I could do but wait. I was caught between my goals and the situation at hand, hoping like hell my chances of getting to talk to the mayor wouldn't slip through my fingers like smoke.

ANOTHER FORTY-FIVE MINUTES PASSED BEFORE I FINALLY sauntered through the lobby, trying not to look like what I'd been through. My diamond cufflinks gleamed under the crystal chandeliers, but my nerves were still worn thin, and I wasn't a nervous nigga. I was over two hours late for the annual prestigious business gala. As I neared the grand ballroom entrance, I caught sight of her: a stunning goddess perched on a plush stool at the bar. Her body and face card had me stuck.

Her skin was the color of rich caramel, reminiscent of Werther's Original candy. She wore a sparkling jet-black gown that hugged every curve with a split that led up her juicy, tatted right thigh. Her long legs were crossed at the knee with heels on her feet. Her brown eyes, framed by long, sweeping lashes, locked onto mine and stopped my heart mid-beat.

I hesitated, torn between obedience and desire. But then, something in her sultry gaze summoned me. Maybe it was the sexy way her lips curved into a teasing smile or her subtle nod while holding her champagne flute. Without a second thought, I veered toward the bar, my heart thumping in my chest.

My look softened as I approached her. Some of me wondered if she could've been the date Jules lined up for me, but with how late I was, something told me otherwise.

"Mind if I join you?" I queried, my voice smoother than aged cognac.

She tilted her head toward me, assessing me from head to toe. Her brown eyes were swirls of amber and cocoa. I wondered what stories hid behind them. Her long curls were adorned with glittering silver hair pins, perfectly framing the right side of her face. My pupils widened, recording every detail of her beauty, from the dip of her cupid's bow on the top of her lips to the slim, almost unnoticeable gap between her two front teeth.

"Be my guest," she replied.

"You here with someone?" I inquired as I waved down the bartender to order a glass of cognac on the rocks, anything to settle my spirit.

"Maybe I'm here for you."

"Your name wouldn't happen to be Kiera, would it?"

The name was the only thing I could remember about my arranged date. I couldn't check in with Jules for an update on a dead cell.

"Cute name. But it's not mine," she confirmed with a soft shrug.

"I'm not tryna sound like a creep, but my assistant set me up with a date for tonight's gala. My cell is dead, and I'm over two hours late. So, I'm thinking by now I've been stood up."

"Two hours? Yeah, she's definitely left your black ass by now. I know I would have."

"Guess I gotta go in there alone then."

She smirked. "You scared? Don't tell me you're all bark and no bite," she teased.

I chuckled, relieved by her sarcastic humor. "Trust me, beautiful. I bite. I'm a lot of things, and a scared nigga ain't one of 'em."

"Noted. I've heard of fashionably late, but are you tardy because you're important or because you're a reckless ass nigga?"

"A bit of both," I admitted. "I'm Ahsan Patton."

She extended her hand. "Bella." Our fingers touched, and it was as if the world around us faded to black.

"Just Bella?"

"Just Bella. Is this event more business or pleasure for you?"

"All business. And what about you?"

"Depends," she replied, her tone playful.

My right brow lurched toward my crisp hairline. "On?"

I studied Bella's beauty, forgetting all about the gala momentarily. Instead, my ass was lost in her cat-shaped eyes, wondering how someone so captivating could be sitting alone. She had a face card that would never decline.

She took her time sipping champagne before parting her red-painted lips to speak. "What do you do anyway?" she questioned, changing the course of our conversation. "Must be pretty important to be a guest, right?"

"I own a trucking company. And yourself?"

"I'm a spy."

"A what?" I queried before taking a sip of my drink.

"What? You don't believe me?"

"Nah. I don't."

"Well, that's too bad for you."

"You're funny, you know that?"

"Hmm. Maybe I should've been a stand-up comedian then."

"I could see you ripping the stage."

"I kind of already do that, just differently. I'm a dancer."

My brows downturned. "A dancer? Like, a stripper or a ballerina?"

She smirked. "That also depends."

I chuckled. "On what this time?"

"How much I'm getting paid," she said boldly.

"What kind of money do you make a night at the club you work at?" I asked, already knowing what type of time she was on.

I may have been in a rush when I entered the hotel, but that didn't stop me from noticing the variety of women scattered throughout the lobby, waiting to be picked up and tricked on by a nigga.

Her lean, caramel shoulders rose and fell. "That's based on the night and who's in the building. I can usually get a few hundred."

"Be specific. What exactly is a few hundred?"

"Like, anywhere from three hundred and fifty to five hundred dollars if it's a good night. But it can differ after splitting with the bouncers and bartenders and giving back a cut to the club."

"And you like what you do?"

"It's not my end goal if that's what you're asking."

I chuckled. "Touché. What is the end goal then?" I inquired, testing her for substance. It would have been a shame if she was all beauty and no brains.

"I'm an artist."

My head tilted to the side. "First, you're a spy, then a dancer, and now an artist. You're a real jack of all trades."

"The spy shit was cap, but everything else was true."

"A real hustler. I fuck with it."

"I don't play about my money."

"Looks like we have something in common."

She agreed with the dip of her rounded chin. "Looks like we do."

I tilted my head back to finish the rest of my drink before turning my body toward hers. "How much for the evening?" I queried boldly, eyes trained on hers.

I'd never been the type of nigga to want or need to rent pussy by the hour, but desperate times called for desperate measures. I could hear Jules's voice telling me how much I'd stand out without a beautiful woman at my side. But as the minutes continued to slip by, I couldn't help but feel that Bella might have been the good luck charm I needed to turn my night around.

Bella swallowed hard before slowly licking her lips. "Step into my office."

BELLA AND I STEPPED INTO THE GRAND BALLROOM ARM IN ARM. The space was bathed in soft lighting from the crystal chandeliers hanging overhead. Her heels clicked against the polished marble floor as we walked through the sea of mingling CEOs, political figures, and tech moguls. Waitstaff dressed in crisp black and white attire circulated the room with trays of champagne, mini lobster rolls, and caviar-topped hors d'oeuvres.

The ballroom buzzed with clinking champagne flutes, laughter, and hushed conversations. Each round table had tealight candles and a towering vase centerpiece overflowing with fresh white orchids. Next to the stage was a live jazz band playing as couples twirled on the dance floor in their shimmering gowns and tailored tuxedos. My eyes darted around, assessing the connections being made and potential opportunities. I spotted the mayor on the dance floor.

I turned to face Bella. "You said you dance, right?" I inquired.

"Yeah. Why?"

"Let me see your moves."

She arched a brow in my direction. "You dance?"

"Only when I'm in the mood."

"So, let me get this straight. You're a baller and a ballroom dancer?"

"Guess we're about to find out."

The jazz band switched the tempo, playing a slow, sultry rendition of "Kiss of Life" by Sade. I led Bella toward the center of the dance floor, stopping only a few feet away from the mayor and his wife. My hand rested on the small of her back. The touch was both possessive and gentle.

Bella's midnight-black gown swirled around her smooth legs as we moved. Her bubbly laughter echoed, causing me to smile wider than I had in a long time. My designer loafers glided across the marble floor as I pulled her closer. Our bodies fit perfectly like two puzzle pieces. Soon, everything in the room faded into insignificance. All that mattered was the warmth of my hand on her small waist and the certainty that our first dance would be the beginning of something sensational.

I spun her, and her giggling turned into a gasp. "Oh shit. You really can dance."

I dipped her low, my breath brushing her ear as I smirked. "I must be in the mood."

An unexpected interruption sliced through our romantic bubble as we swayed in each other's arms, lost in our private thoughts. I looked up to see Mayor Dinkins a few heartbeats away from me, and I froze mid-step.

"Mr. Patton," the mayor's voice cut through the music. "Good to see you."

"Good to see you too, Mayor Dinkins. I was hoping to get a minute of your time to discuss my business proposal. Can we talk?"

Bella's gaze flickered from me to the mayor. She stepped back and allowed her fingers to slip from mine. Duty called, and I had no choice but to follow. As I walked away, I glanced back at her and made a silent promise that the mayor's interruption wouldn't be the end of our story.

Sienna

Being with Ahsan made me feel like Cinderella at the ball. And as the clock struck midnight, a part of me wasn't ready for my carriage to turn back into a pumpkin. I'd never been so captivated by a nigga's presence before. His touch was both confident and gentle. His laughter was a low rumble like a summer thunderstorm. And when he spoke, his words were expressive like poetry, yet commanding like a gangsta. He was successful, charming, and light on his feet, all wrapped up in one fine-ass milk chocolate bow. Ahsan's tailored tux clung to his broad shoulders, signaling wealth and power. His brown skin was a rich shade of milk chocolate, displaying the warmth of sun-kissed days. My gaze traced the sharp angles of his jaw, his full beard shadowing his skin. His dark brown eyes were deep and mysterious, like the depths of the ocean. I didn't know anything about him besides his name, and I didn't care. All that mattered was he was a certified boss.

He stepped away, leaving me in the center of the dance floor. I didn't know what business he had to discuss with the mayor, but I knew it was important by the serious look on his face and the way he'd quickly disappeared into the crowd. My black gown clung to my curves, its sequined fabric gleaming as I shifted my weight from one heel to the other. The soothing sounds of the jazz band hummed in the background. Guests, dressed to the nines, swirled around me, lost in the sultry rhythm of the music. My eyes scanned the ballroom and stopped when I spotted a regal woman walking toward me. She greeted me with a knowing smile as her expensive perfume wafted past my nostrils.

"Men," she said, her voice low. "Always running off to attend to business."

I shrugged. "Never a dull moment."

The woman, who I assumed was the mayor's wife, chuckled. "Exactly. You'd think I'd be used to it after almost thirty years."

She was the epitome of poise. Her silver-streaked hair was swept into a curly updo, and a string of pearls decorated her neck. Her silk, sky-blue gown clung to her slender frame, its neckline modest for her age. Her brown eyes held a lifetime of wisdom, and her smile was genuine.

My brows heightened toward my baby hair. "Wow. That's longer than I've been alive."

"Tell me, my dear," she said, leaning in. "How long have you and your date been together?"

I hesitated to relay the truth on my tongue as my gaze drifted toward the grand double doors where Ahsan had disappeared. "We just met tonight, actually," I confessed.

"Tonight? The way you two were sweeping around the dance floor, I would've thought you'd known each other for decades."

"I guess we just click like that."

"Call me a hopeless romantic, but that sounds like soulmates to me."

Before I could respond, the crowd shifted, revealing Ahsan and the mayor's return. My heart skipped a beat as Ahsan sauntered toward me, his steps guided. His eyes found mine, and just like that, the room blurred, leaving only the two of us with a dance to resume.

He held out his hand for mine. The warmth of his unfamiliar yet invited touch ignited goosebumps along my exposed caramel skin. "Forgive my absence," he muttered, his voice smooth like velvet. "Business shit, you know."

My lips curved into a smirk. "It's fine," I replied. "I kept myself occupied while you were gone."

"Oh yeah?" he queried, drawing me in close. His thumb brushed my knuckles as our bodies fit together like a hand in a glove. His touch was firm yet gentle as he guided my steps. His calloused fingers found the small of my back with ease. I leaned into him, my body yielding, trusting. The heat of his palm seeped through the fabric of my gown, igniting a spark that surged up my spine.

"I even made a new friend."

"Who?"

I traced the lapel of his tuxedo, the fabric smooth underneath my fingertips. "The mayor's wife."

"Forreal?"

"Yeah. She seems to think we've been a couple for years. She was shocked when I told her we'd just met tonight."

"First dates are always stressful," he said, his voice a low rumble that resonated through my body.

I smirked. "Too bad this isn't a date. It's a business arrangement, remember?"

We'd agreed on five hundred dollars for me to accompany him to the gala. I ensured we hit the ATM before entering the ballroom, so I got my money upfront.

"And how you feelin' about that?"

I gazed into his eyes with a whirlwind of emotions twisting my insides. His irises held the promise of dollar signs with a hint of desire. Lust simmered beneath his fingertips as he held my waist, a slow-burning flame that threatened to consume all reason if they inched down toward my ass. I couldn't help but wonder if he felt it, too—the heat of the moment.

Curiosity danced in my chest with a flurry of questions: *Does he have a wife or girlfriend at home somewhere barefoot and pregnant?*

What stories are hiding behind his mysterious brown eyes? I shook my head, ridding the thoughts of a fairy-tale romance from my mind. We weren't a couple. We were strangers. We didn't go way back like four flats. When the evening ended, so would our arrangement.

"I should be the one asking you that. You're the one who paid. Do you think you made a good investment?"

"So far, so good. But ask me again at the end of the night," he replied with a smirk.

I chuckled. "Will do."

"So, earlier, you said you're an artist."

I nodded, my smile revealing a hint of vulnerability. "Yes. I paint."

"Tell me about your favorite piece," he said before gently spinning me around.

"Well, right now, I'd say my series called *Soul Ties*. It was recently selected for next month's exhibition at the Gallery at Forestbrook."

"Soul ties? Sounds deep as fuck."

"It is. I want my art to evoke emotions that linger in people's hearts whenever they look at my work. And who knows, maybe even change a few of them, too."

He dipped me low, and my breath hitched as I clung to him. Our eyes locked, and we were suspended in time for a fleeting second. "You wanna change the world?"

"I'll settle for a piece of it," I whispered.

"And congratulations on your exhibit. You're excited about it, right?"

I nodded. "Honestly, I'm ecstatic."

"Then flaunt that shit like a badge of honor. Be proud of what you accomplished, and never dim your light. There are too many mothafuckas in the world ready and willing to do that for you," he stated, dropping a million dollars' worth of game on me for free.

"You're right. I'm just sensitive about my shit, so it means a lot to me that someone saw my talent. After dropping out, I've been fighting hard to return to art school. So, I've just been in this gray area of excitement and imposter syndrome ever since I got the news."

I had no idea why I was openly venting to a stranger about my art or my feelings, but I couldn't stop. Something about Ahsan had allowed a part of me to bloom and open up unexpectedly.

"And you said you own a trucking company, right?"

"Yeah."

"What's the story behind that?"

He guided me into a smooth turn. When I spun away, my laughter filled the space between us before my chest pressed against his. I felt the rhythm of our heartbeats align. "I started it about eight years back with a single truck, hauling goods nationwide. Now I've got a fleet."

"Wow. That's impressive. And you're how old?"

"I'll be thirty-five in a few months. I still remember the day the man handed me the keys to my first truck. It was freedom, responsibility, and power all rolled into one."

"Is that what you wanted to talk to the mayor about? Your trucking business? Not to be nosy or anything. It looked important, that's all," I replied.

"It was."

"Did it go well?"

"It did. Thank you." His smile held both mischief and vulnerability.

"You're welcome."

As we spun around the dance floor, the gala became our backdrop. I couldn't help but wonder if there would be more to our night or if it would end once the music did. Would I be okay with either outcome? Or was I holding onto hope in vain?

THE EVENT ENDED A COUPLE OF HOURS LATER, AND THE DIMLY lit bar where we'd first met welcomed us back. Rich mahogany wood panels decorated the walls filled with hundreds of liquor bottles. Above our heads were black and gold pendant lights that cast a soft glow against the polished bar top. Ahsan ordered a cognac neat, and I chose a crisp white wine. We settled onto barstools and clinked our glasses together in a toast before I looked around. I hadn't seen Zyon since we arrived at the hotel together and split up. In fact, I hadn't seen anyone but Ahsan in hours.

"Thank you for coming with me tonight, Bella. I hope you enjoyed yourself."

"I mean, it's not like I volunteered my time. You paid me to come, but I did have fun. Better than expected," I admitted.

"That's a good thing, right?" he queried as he sipped his drink.

"It's a great thing. I didn't know what I was going to get myself into when I stepped foot in here a few hours ago. So, let's just say spending the evening being twirled around the dance floor by the handsomest nigga in the room was a pleasant surprise."

"You weren't so bad on that dance floor yourself. It takes a lot to surprise me, and you did."

"How so?" I quizzed, sweeping my curls behind my ear.

"A woman with natural beauty, talent, and brains is hard to come by."

"Or maybe you've just been looking in all the wrong places."

"I haven't been looking at all."

"And why is that?"

"My business and desire to make money have always been my top priorities."

"Hustle to avoid the heartbreak. I get it."

"Something told me you would," he said, swirling the amber liquor in his glass. "So, tell me more about your upcoming art exhibit."

My eyes danced with life just thinking about it. "It's my first one," I confessed. "It's at a small gallery downtown. I can't wait to see my work on display. I'm sure I'll probably drown in a puddle of tears."

He traced the rim of his glass. "I'd love to see your work."

My smile widened. "Really?"

"I can see the hunger for recognition in your eyes. I recognize it in myself. Besides, I've got a few pieces in my condo already, but I'm looking for more to hang on those bare walls."

"Sounds like divine timing," I said. "Maybe I'll send you an invite, and if you like what you see, maybe my work can find a new home with you."

"I was thinking of something custom."

"Like what?"

Ahsan leaned closer. "You tell me. You said you want your work to draw out emotions, right? I want you to paint me something that speaks to you. I want each stroke to tell a story."

The way the word *stroke* fell off his tongue made me clench my thighs together. I cleared my throat before taking a small sip of my wine. "Emotions on canvas. Got it."

"Let's exchange numbers, and when you have something for me, you let me know."

"Is this a slick way for you to get my number?" I quizzed, lurching my brow upward.

"I thought this was all business."

I agreed. "It is."

"Okay, then."

"As long as we're both on the same page."

I could tell he wanted more, and maybe deep down, a part of me did, too. But in the meantime, things between Ahsan and I were all business, not personal.

"And speaking of business, I'm not sure I'm ready for the night to end," Ahsan admitted.

My heart skipped a beat. "Oh?"

"How much to make you mine the rest of the night?" he asked boldly, cutting straight to the chase before finishing the liquor in his glass.

I cleared my throat again, trying to buy myself time to think of an answer. I hadn't had to set a price before because I'd never sold my pussy. He'd handed over the five hundred dollars with ease earlier. I was curious to see how much more he'd come off of.

"A G," I replied.

"One thousand dollars?"

I shrugged. "No such thing as a free lunch. My price is my price."

Ahsan dipped his chin. "Fair enough. Let me get the money and a room, and I'll be back."

I raised my glass, ecstatic that I'd been able to make a full month's rent in one night without having to share my earnings with anyone. "To future business arrangements."

"To future business arrangements," he repeated as we clinked glasses.

AHSAN PAID FOR A ROOM, AND WE ENTERED THE ELEVATOR TO the sixteenth floor. I was his for the night. I didn't exactly know what that meant, but telling by the way his hand hadn't left my waist since we'd stepped inside the metal box, I was sure I was bound to find out. We stood close, our fragrances mingling—my airy perfume with the scent of his expensive-smelling cologne. The elevator slowed, and the doors cracked open. We lingered for a second, my heartbeat suspended.

His thumb brushed the small of my back. "Let's go."

I gasped the moment I stepped into the room. I'd never been in anything so lavish. The walls were champagne-colored and ornamented with gold mirrors. The king bed in the center of the room was adorned with crisp white sheets with a thread count I couldn't wait to feel against my skin. The vaulted ceiling and floor-to-ceiling windows revealed a breathtaking view of the Vegas Strip.

"Wow. This view is everything."

"You ever been in a room this nice before?" he inquired.

"No. Never. But I'm sure you do shit like this all the time."

"I rarely visit hotels," he answered.

His response triggered another question in my brain. "You ever done this before?"

"What? Pick up a beautiful woman in a bar?"

"Pay her," I clarified.

"No. You?"

"You want the truth?"

"Nothing but," he said while sliding off his tuxedo jacket.

"It's my first time too. Not the fucking, just the money part," I clarified. "And Bella isn't my real name. It's my stage name."

"What's your real name?"

"Sienna."

He studied me hard as if trying to read my innermost thoughts. "Any more secrets you wanna share, Sienna?"

I swung my head to the left. "No."

"Good. Anything you wanna know about me?"

I hesitated. "Do you have a wife or girlfriend?"

"After what I've just paid you, do you care?"

"Not really."

"Good."

My breath hitched as he pulled me close. I leaned into his touch, my eyes closing briefly, savoring our electric connection. His lips brushed mine, and in that stolen breath, I surrendered to the mystery behind his eyes and the magic of the night.

"Let me go freshen up. I'll be right back."

A few minutes later, I stepped out wearing a matching red bra and panty set that accentuated my slender stomach and petite curves. The four-inch heels on my feet elongated my height as I sauntered over to him. Ahsan's eyes caught mine as he sat on the edge of the king-sized bed, legs spread wide. When our gazes collided, it was as if the room blurred for a second.

I stood between his legs, feeling completely in control as if I were at the club giving a private dance. I swayed my hips, letting them sing the hypnotizing tune that made a nigga feel like he was the only one in the room. I knew how to make a nigga dream a little dream of me, at least for the duration of a song. Our unwavering eye contact was a silent conversation within itself. It was a dance of curiosity and lust that kept my undivided attention. I reached out to wrap my hands around his neck while straddling him. I gently started gyrating my hips against him while peppering soft kisses against his neck.

I was intoxicated by the faint aroma of expensive cologne against his skin. He slid his hands down the small of my back, stopping underneath my ass before he kissed me. Feeling Ahsan's soft lips against mine didn't unlock a new level of physical connection between us, but an emotional one that vibrated throughout my entire body. I unbuttoned his dress shirt while he massaged my hips and ass. A moan slipped past my lips the minute I felt him slide my panties to the side.

"Mmm, shit, that pussy is leaking for a nigga already," he growled, breath cool against my ear.

"Before we go any further... safety first," I whispered, pointing to the Magnum box hanging from my purse on the nightstand.

"Bet."

I crawled across the bed and pulled off one condom from the three pack. Ahsan stood to his feet and inched over to me. I handed him the condom. He pulled me to the edge of the bed before forcefully bending me over and pulling my panties down to my ankles before smacking my ass. I looked over my shoulder, watching as he unbuckled his dress trousers and pulled his wife beater over his head, revealing the giant face of a lion tattoo stretching across his chest. I bit my lip. He was a sexy ass mothafucka. His handsome face and rock-hard, tattooed abs made my yoni weep. I had a weakness for bad boys with big bankrolls, and Ahsan was my kryptonite. It was as if God himself had painted his melanated perfection into existence. I watched him bite the edge of the gold wrapper, tearing off a piece before pulling out the condom and rolling it over the tip of his stiffened rod.

I turned over and sat up on my knees. I planted kisses down his tattooed chest, stopping to kiss and lick his nipples before inching down each of his eight abs. I held his hips while gliding my tongue up and down his shaft. I focused my mouth game on his thick, mushroom-shaped tip.

"Mmm shit," he growled, gripping a fistful of my curls.

I held his Magnum-molded dick by the base and bobbed my head up and down. Next came spitting on the head while massaging his smooth, chocolate balls. I let the spit hang from my lips while flashing my eyes at him. His brooding gaze pierced mine as I opened my mouth wide before giving the tip of his dick mouth to mouth. He looked at me through his deep pools of cocoa with a mix of lust and pleasure.

Ahsan sucked in air through his teeth before biting down on his bottom lip. His grip on my hair remained tight as I twisted and slid my hands up and down his pole.

"Fuck, come here and ride this dick."

Ahsan's dick stood at attention as I eased down onto it. I rocked forward and backward while sliding up and down his rod like an on-duty firefighter.

"Oh shit! Yes! Mmm, shit!" I squealed as he thrust his hips upward inside me.

Our bodies spoke without words, and our souls swirled, blending our colors into the perfect shade. It was like fate had drawn our souls together, and the universe was pulling us closer.

I hunched forward, wildly thrusting and bucking my hips. Ahsan's hands fondled my breasts and held my throat. I leaned my head back and spread my ass cheeks apart while he choked and fucked me deep.

I moaned loudly. "Oh shit. Right there! Don't stop!"

I firmly pressed my palms into his chest as he gripped a handful of my curls and forced my lips onto his. His tongue explored the depths of my throat. I arched my back as his hands found my waist, holding on as I rolled my hips. He pushed his knees up behind me so that I could feel him in my stomach.

"Oh my God! Yes! I'm cumming!"

"Cum, Sienna. Cum all over this dick. You can make as much mess as you want," Ahsan confirmed before kissing me through my climax.

Ahsan had my pussy running like a faucet. I was happy he'd given me "permission" to leak all over him. "Oooh fuck! Fuck! Fuck! Yes!"

"Now turn that sexy ass over."

I complied, panting heavily. The dick was spectacular. It felt so good I couldn't help but smile. Ahsan widened his stance, stationing one foot on the floor while the other was mounted on top of the bed for leverage. He pushed me face down into the sheets and gripped my hips so that my back was arched and my ass was poked up.

He slid his snake back inside my warmth and wasted no time delivering long, hard strokes. Ahsan rested one hand on my lower back with the other on my nape.

I licked my lips while pushing my hair out of my face. He pulled out of me then grabbed my ankles and pulled me to the edge of the bed like a rag doll before dipping back inside me. His palm smacked my ass before he bucked harder, pressing his chest against my back and burying himself deep inside my guts.

Ahsan kissed my neck before grabbing a handful of my curls and yanking my head back. "Open those pretty fucking eyes of yours," he commanded.

My lids lifted, and I stuck out my tongue, all but begging for him to kiss me. His sexy ass obliged me by leaning forward and slipping his tongue inside my mouth. He pulled me up onto my knees and hooked my arms behind my back before dicking me the hell down. I looked over my shoulder at him, watching him smack my jiggling ass.

"That's it. Throw that shit back like you 'posed to," Ahsan commanded with beads of sweat sliding down his forehead as he bit his bottom lip. I'd never seen a sexier sight.

Switching positions, I lay on my back. Our bodies entwined, our chemistry a fusion of craving and release. Our bare chests pressed together, and our fingers interlocked as our bodies spoke to each other in a language only his dick and my pussy could understand. He fit inside me like a lock and key.

Ahsan gripped my smooth calf as my leg dangled over his shoulder. His thumb stroked my clit, making my legs shake with pleasure before he pushed his dick back inside me.

"Mmm, goddamn," he growled, slapping my freely jiggling breasts.

He pushed my knees toward my chest, and I hooked my hands underneath my legs to hold them in place while he drilled into me. I felt our orbits intersecting with each long, deep stroke. He kept a steady rhythm while pressing his palms against the back of my thighs.

I gripped the sheets as I watched his brick-hard dick snake in and out of me. My toes curled as my back arched toward the ceiling. I palmed the back of his waves, pulling him close as he thrust hard and deep, inching toward his climax. I held the back of his thighs, forcing him deeper into me.

"Ohhhh shit," he groaned, cumming with his hand around my throat and his eyes closed, lost in euphoria.

Ahsan rolled over beside me, chest quickly rising and falling. He twisted his neck toward me, admiring my naked body. "A thousand wasn't nearly enough, Sienna. What you got between those thighs is worth millions."

Ahsan

I gripped the brass handle and pushed open the heavy oak door to my office building before walking inside. The rejuvenating aroma of freshly brewed coffee wafted through the air, courtesy of the espresso machine near Jules's desk. The walls were adorned with framed certificates and accolades, a legitimate testament to my company's success. Jules sat at her desk, her mocha brown fingers tapping rhythmically on her keyboard. She glanced up from her computer screen, her expression a mix of confusion and content. She'd always been able to read me like a book.

"Ahsan," she said, her voice upbeat like a melody.

"Wassup, Jules?"

"You already know I have a million questions for you! What the hell happened on Saturday?"

"Good morning to you too."

"Yeah, yeah. Come on! Spill the tea. What the hell went on at that gala?"

"What makes you think something went down?"

"Um, because the woman I set you up with said you never

showed. Plus, the mayor's office called first thing this morning. They want to set up a meeting to talk about your proposal."

I sighed. "She said I didn't show up because I was two hours late getting there, and my phone died."

She arched an eyebrow. "Late? That's not like you."

"Yeah, well, traffic was a fucking nightmare with all the detours, and I didn't have a charger."

"So, what happened when you finally got there?"

"I went to the gala, spoke to the mayor, and that was that."

She folded her arms across her chest. "That's it?"

I chuckled while crossing the room to stand by the window. "What do you want me to say? The gala was a blur. People in tuxes and gowns dancing and sipping champagne. But it wasn't the event that stole my attention."

Jules leaned back in her chair, intrigued by my comment. "What then?"

I turned to face her, my gaze steady. "Her."

"*Her?*" Jules quizzed, a twinge of jealousy in her voice. "Why the hell are you being so cryptic right now?"

The office door creaked open before I could provide details, and Amir stepped inside. His retro sneakers squeaked against the hardwood floor. I glanced up, surprise flickering across my face as I reached out to dap him up. "Wassup, bro?"

"Sup, Ahsan. Hey, Jules," he greeted us.

"Hey, Amir. Get comfy. Your brother was just about to tell me about the woman who had his nose wide open on Saturday," Jules informed him, bringing him up to speed.

"Hold up? What now?" Amir queried, leaning on the side of Jules's desk.

I sucked my teeth. "All I'm saying is, it all worked out how it was supposed to."

"What does that mean?" Jules pressed.

"You said the mayor's office called, didn't you? I spoke with him, and I found a date."

Her fingers drummed on the desk. "You *what?*"

"Yeah."

"Who was she?" Amir quizzed.

"She's an artist."

His brow creased. "Since when you like an artsy fartsy type of bitch?"

I cut him a hard glare. "Yo, chill with all that. She's incredible."

"What's her name?" Jules probed.

"Sienna," I answered, liking that ten times more than her stage name.

"Sienna the artist. And you met this broad where?"

"At the bar in the hotel that night. We struck up a conversation, and one thing led to another, and she joined me. That's it. End of story," I confirmed, hoping to put an end to their suspicions.

Amir chuckled with a scoff. "Yeah, okay."

The phone rang, sending Jules over to answer it. Amir followed me into my office and closed the door behind him. "So, wassup, nigga? Who is she really?"

"What you mean? I told you."

"You told me the PG version for Jules. Now I want the explicit details."

"You a nasty nigga, you know that?"

"Me? You the one with that junkie itch, nigga. How bad she put it on you?"

I sighed before folding my body into my office chair. "Shit, nigga. We danced like we owned the room all night. I couldn't tear myself away from her. But a nigga not sprung if that's what you're saying."

His lips curved into a knowing smile. "Yeah, all right. So what now?"

I shrugged. The mayor's office lingered in the back of my mind. But I could genuinely say my thoughts were elsewhere for the first time in forever. I wondered if Sienna felt the same magnetic force that pulled us together.

"I'll have Jules set up a meeting with the mayor's office, but as far as Sienna..." My voice trailed off as I became lost in the memory of the night we shared. "I don't know. Maybe it might be the right time to detract from my plan."

"So, that's what it takes to get you to give up that plan? Some good pussy?"

I sucked my teeth. "Shut your ass up, nigga. I'm cool. Fuck you come here for anyway?"

"To talk about the next shipment."

"What about it? We can't have another issue like we had with the Houston shipment. We took a big hit."

"Real professionals understand shipping issues," he reminded me. "It's not like that shit happens all the time."

"I know, but I've got an eerie feeling. It's been in the pit of his stomach for weeks now. I know something is coming. I'm just not sure when or where."

Amir scoffed. "That's your paranoia talking, nigga."

"Fuck that. Let's bulk up security around the warehouse and stash houses and change our trucking routes. If you plan to still expand into Texas once I step down, we need to be cautious," I said, knowing that in our line of work, niggas didn't have a long shelf life.

"All right, bet." He agreed with a nod.

"Loop in Rico and Bradley on the changes," I said, mentioning our lieutenants overseeing our stash houses. "For now, I need you and XL to take over the day-to-day operations while I shake this shit out with the mayor's office. I gotta keep my hands clean as a whistle right now."

Amir reached out to dap me up. "I got you."

Sienna

The steam from the shower clung to my freshly washed skin as I stepped onto the cool tiles of the bathroom floor. Droplets raced down my lean shoulders, tracing the rod of my spine as I reached for my towel hanging on the back of the door. My phone chimed on the sink, slicing through the silence. The screen lit up with a message from Ahsan, the man who'd unexpectedly taken my breath away at the gala.

AHSAN: *Have you painted something for me yet?*

My eyes scanned the screen, and I plopped down on the toilet seat, considering my response. The truth was, I hadn't. At least not yet. I needed to understand his tastes better to capture the essence of his blend of success and rough edges before I could create something custom for him. Simply put, I needed to know what made him tick.

ME: *Not yet. I need to know more about your tastes to find inspiration.*

I typed back, my stiletto-shaped nails tapping on the screen. His reply came almost instantly.

AHSAN: *Say less.*

I chuckled. Ahsan was direct and unapologetic as hell. It

intrigued me. A few seconds later, he followed up with another message.

AHSAN: *I need you for a few hours tonight. How much for your time?*

ME: *What exactly did you have in mind?*

AHSAN: *Early dinner tonight. Wear comfortable shoes. Drop your address and your price. I'll pick you up at six sharp.*

Anticipation fluttered in my chest. *How much would I charge? Where were we going? What the fuck was the occasion?*

"Shit," I mumbled, shooting up from the toilet to pace the floor inside the small bathroom. I was far from a master negotiator. "What the fuck do I say?"

I thought about asking Zyon, but I hadn't even brought him up to her since we'd met. For the moment, I wanted to keep everything, even the thought of him, all to myself. I huffed. I was on my own. He'd already told me my pussy was worth millions, so I knew I wouldn't be able to keep him off me if he was given the chance. Hell, I secretly couldn't wait to feel his body on mine again. It was all I'd been thinking about since it went down. But the fact that there was a transaction behind it, I wouldn't dare let myself get too wrapped up in what could be.

"Future business arrangements, remember, Sienna?" I said to my reflection in the misty mirror. *Plus, we've got back rent to pay and groceries to buy.* "Okay, okay. I got this."

ME: *Five thousand. That's for me and your custom art. 7189 Cheshire Boulevard, Apartment 7C. Text me when you're outside. I'll come down.*

AHSAN: *I'll see you soon.*

My eyes ballooned as my heart galloped in my chest. "Holy fucking shit! He agreed! He actually fucking agreed!" I squealed before darting my eyes up to the top of my screen to catch the time. I had two hours to get ready.

I stepped outside the bathroom and went into my room to get dressed. Thoughts darted through my mind, wondering what he had planned for our evening. Maybe I'd find the inspiration I was looking for behind his eyes and brooding expression, or perhaps I'd find something else that would make my pulse quicken.

***

Ahsan arrived promptly, his knuckles colliding with my apartment door at six sharp as promised. My heart quickened. *What the fuck is he doing at my door? I told him I'd come outside.* I swung open the door, and his eyes instantly penetrated mine. He wore a lime green Dior T-shirt with gold chains hanging over the round neck. His light-washed jeans were distressed at the knees, and the white, brown, and neon green designer sneakers on his feet completed his ensemble.

He looked me up and down, assessing my attire. I wore baggy Levi jeans with rips in the knees, a black lace bralette, a cropped leather jacket, and high-top Converses with my hoop earrings and hair pulled back into a high, sleek ponytail.

I looked down at my clothes. "Am I dressed appropriately for the occasion, or do I need to change?"

"You look perfect." His gaze transferred from me to the unfinished canvases propped up on the easel by the window. "Impressive," he complimented, his voice low and gravelly.

My eyes shot toward the ground. I didn't know how I could simultaneously feel grateful and vulnerable for the flattery. It was like he was seeing my naked soul in those unfinished pieces, yet he seemed to have an eye for detail. "Thanks...You ready to go?"

Instead of responding, he stepped inside and walked over closer, studying every stroke, every raw edge, and every emotion in my half-finished pieces.

"What's this one called?" he asked, studying the one on the easel.

"It's called *Pretty Hurts.* It's supposed to be an interpretation of how one person's beauty can be another person's pain."

"And why haven't you finished it?" he inquired.

I slowly swung my head. "I don't know."

"Why don't you know?"

"I told you I'm sensitive about my shit. I feel like I'm standing naked in front of you right now, and it's making my skin crawl!" I admitted as my chest deflated with a hard sigh.

Ahsan smirked devilishly. "Wouldn't be the first time."

I felt my cheeks burning with embarrassment. "Oh my God! Can we please go?"

He belted out a soft chuckle. "Fine. Let's go."

We stepped out of my apartment building and walked over to his burgundy G-wagon truck. It was sleek on chrome wheels, matching the swag that clung to him like a second shadow. We settled inside against the leather seats, and I fastened my seat belt. My curiosity got the best of me and bubbled right out of my mouth.

"Where are we going?" I queried, my fingers tapping nervously against my thigh.

Ahsan's full lips curved into a half-smile. "Baseball field," he replied. "I need to blow off some steam."

"Baseball?" I quizzed, my mind spinning a web of scenarios.

"Yeah, baseball."

It wasn't what I'd expected to fall off his tongue, but nothing about Ahsan had been predictable since I met him. I leaned back, watching the city blur outside the passenger window. I imagined him teaching me how to swing a bat, our bodies nestled close, the scent of grass and dirt enveloping us. The truck hummed as he revved the engine, accelerating faster down the road. As he drove, I stole glances at him, soaking in the fullness of his bearded jaw and the way his curved fingers gripped the steering wheel. Baseball field or not, I knew I was in for an eventful night.

THIRTY MINUTES LATER, THE BASEBALL FIELD STRETCHED OUT before us, a painted canvas of green and brown under the hot evening sun. The smell of freshly mowed grass surrounded me as we stepped onto the diamond. The bases lay spread against the dirt with what looked like hundreds of feet away. I imagined players sprinting in their cleats across the soil as they hit every base, destined for a home run. I looked to the outfield bordered by a chain-link fence then the scoreboard and empty bleachers encircling the field. I could almost hear the distant roaring of the cheering crowd as they urged their favorite team to win. Near the dugout on the first-base side of the field was a table set for two decorated with a crisp white tablecloth, a wicker picnic basket, floating tealight candles, and various vases filled with red roses.

"Where is everyone? We're the only ones here." I observed as Ahsan led me to the center field, where the grass seemed to stretch for miles.

"I rented out the entire space to ensure our privacy," he answered, as if the cost to rent out an entire baseball stadium was pennies.

I turned to him, my heart thundering. "Seriously?"

"Yeah. You said you wanted to get to know a nigga more, right?"

"Right, but I—"

"No buts."

I couldn't believe he'd rented the whole fucking stadium out, let alone planned out an elaborate date night for us. The chain-link fence encircled us like a cocoon, and the sounds of the pulsing city were replaced with the chirping of crickets and the hum of the bright stadium lights.

"What the fuck is going on here?"

"What do you mean?"

"First, I throw a wild ass price at you, and you breeze over it like it's nothing. Then you show up at my apartment door, knowing damn well I told you I'd meet you outside. Then you bring me to this big ass fucking baseball stadium and have this romantic ass date planned like you're the black Prince Charming or something."

"And?"

"And? What the fuck do you want from me, Ahsan? What is all this for? I know you have better things to do with your time and your money than to trick out on me."

"You can't tell me how to make my money, and you definitely can't tell me how to spend it. If I wanna ball out on you, Sienna, I'll very well fucking do that shit."

I heard the bite in his voice, and I knew he had that dog in him. I wasn't about to test his gangster, especially when I hadn't been paid yet. "Fine. So, we're here. You gon' show me how to hit a ball or something?"

Ahsan picked up a wooden bat from the ground and handed it to me. The grooves in the handle felt smooth under my palms. His steps toward me were deliberate, swiftly shrinking the distance between us. We were close enough to share the same breathing space, but I held my breath in the charged silence. Ahsan's presence enveloped me. Our connection was like a magnetic pull that defied all rhyme or reason.

"Hold it like this," he instructed, hovering over me from behind. His fingers brushed mine to adjust my grip on the bat. His gentle touch was warm like the sun against my skin. "And when you swing that shit, make sure you follow through. Before you even hit it, already start to imagine the ball's path and how far you'll make that bitch soar like a rocket."

I looked over my shoulder at him and caught him staring at the curve of my lips. Baseball may have been the excuse for us to get close, but the real game was being played in his stolen glances and the electric charge that flickered whenever our bodies touched. My heart raced as I stared back at the baseball pitching machine ahead of me.

"O-Okay."

The first ball came in a white blur, hurling toward me. I closed my eyes and swung, hearing the sharp crack of the baseball hitting the wooden bat ricocheting through the air. My eyes popped open to see the ball soaring through the sky before landing in the grass a few feet away. It was my first perfect swing. I belted out a giggle, feeling the rush of excitement and adrenaline surge through my veins.

"Holy shit, I did it! I actually hit it!"

"Impressive," Ahsan muttered, his cocoa-brown eyes ablaze with genuine approval. "You've got a strong swing."

Our gaze lingered on each other, another brush of intimacy through silent glances. There was recognition behind his eyes as if he were undressing me. My thoughts unraveled. My fingers itched with a primal desire to touch him, to feel the warmth of his body against mine again. I fantasized about tracing the contours of his beard or adorning his handsome seat of a face with my pussy.

I swallowed hard. "Thank you."

"My turn."

Ahsan took the bat and stepped up, his stance confident as if he could hit a ball with one eye closed and one hand tied behind his back. The handle fit snugly in his grasp as if it were a natural extension of his arm. He adjusted his stance just as the machine spit out the ball. He swung, effortlessly connecting with the ball whizzing toward him and sending it flying toward the outfield.

"Why baseball?" I probed, curious about his backstory.

"Baseball has been my escape since I was a kid," he shared while passing the bat back to me.

I studied him with intrigue. "So that's how you learned to hit the ball like a seasoned pro?"

"Baseball teaches you how to deal with pressure. Pressure can make even the smartest nigga make a stupid mistake. The more you play, the better you become at dealing with it, and the calmer you'll be in stressful situations off the field. It teaches you how to be precise and not make emotional decisions."

"You said you wanted to blow off some steam, right? What's got you all worked up?"

"I've got to make a hard decision."

"Which is?"

"Whether or not to take my grandmother off life support. The hospital has been blowing my phone up for the past few days, pressing for an answer," he explained.

"This doesn't sound like something you rush."

"It isn't. But she's been in a coma for weeks with no signs of brain activity."

I lowered my gaze. "I'm sorry to hear that."

"Thank you. She raised me, my brother, and my cousin. None of us want to see her go, but I'm her power of attorney. I have the final say."

"And what say you?" I queried.

Ahsan turned toward me, his gaze softening as the sun began to set. "I say we have to let her go, but my brother and cousin don't want to. I just don't want to make a selfish decision, and I feel like keeping her on the machine just prolongs the inevitable, y'know?"

"Have you all said your goodbyes?"

"Yeah. We have. I'm at peace with it. It's only one way out this mothafucka, and nobody makes it out alive."

"You said she raised you. Where were your parents?"

"My mama and my auntie were strung out on crack bad back in the day, so that's why Big Mama took us in. As far as my dad, the only father figure I've ever known is the streets," he answered before stepping up to hit the ball again.

The bat sliced through the air, kissing the ball with a smack. Another surge of excitement rushed through me. I could've watched him hit balls across the field all night.

"You're a product of the streets turned success story, huh?"

He chuckled. "I guess so. So, what about you? What's your story?"

My shoulders rose and fell with a shrug. "There's not much to know about me."

"I doubt that. Tell me about your family. Did you grow up with a crackhead for a mother like me, or were you tucked away somewhere in the suburbs?"

"I'm a city girl, born and raised in Miami. I moved out here with my cousin, Zyon. And no, I don't talk to my mother like that. She ain't no crackhead. We just don't see eye-to-eye like that. And as far as my father, he left the picture before I could even spell father, so I guess you can't miss what you never had," I stated.

"I feel that way about my pops too. I met him for the first time at my mother's funeral. He got popped three days later. I was seven."

I lowered my gaze out of respect. "Damn."

"You said the night we met was your first time selling pussy, but how long have you been a dancer?"

I frowned. "What is this, an interview? I didn't know I was a celebrity."

He chuckled. "Touché."

"I started dancing when I was twenty-one. I'm twenty-four now," I answered.

"Twenty-four? You've still got Similac on your breath."

I rolled my eyes toward the purplish sky above. "Whatever. How old are you then if I'm a baby?"

"I'll be thirty-five in a few months."

My brows heightened. "Damn. Okay, zaddy," I teased.

He chuckled. "Yo, chill with all that. You hungry?"

The sun's hues dimmed from bright yellow to a deep golden orange as it sank below the horizon. The shadows lengthened across the field, and the dust in the air surrounding us grew visible as I held my hand up to block the power of bright light. "I could eat."

Ahsan led me to the decorated table where our luxury picnic awaited. The scent of fresh bread and cheese wafted from inside the wicker basket. He opened it and pulled out the contents. The spread was basic yet elegant: fresh strawberries, sliced baguette with creamy brie, and a bottle of champagne with two flutes. Ahsan popped the cork and poured the bubbling liquid into our glasses.

We sat side by side, fingers brushing as we reached for the same piece of bread. "You put all this together yourself?"

"I may have had some help."

"From?"

"My assistant. I tell her what I want, and nine times out of ten, she makes it happen."

"Well, she has immaculate taste. Tell her I said thanks." I set my glass on the table and noticed a fat money roll beside one of the vases. "Is this—"

"Your payment," he answered, finishing my sentence for me.

"I still can't believe you paid it."

My pupils instantly turned into dollar signs as I mentally started spending the money before I'd even put it in my hand. I was hypnotized by the lure of the roll of big-faced bills. I reached out and cradled it like I was holding a Big Mac. The texture was crisp and cool to the touch.

"You got plans for it?"

"What? The money?"

"Yeah."

"How'd you know?"

"I can see the hunger in your eyes."

I blinked as if that would wipe away the evidence. "Yeah, well, we can't all be as financially blessed as you. Some of us have bills."

"So, that's what's got you putting a price tag on that pretty ass pussy of yours?"

The edges of his words were sharp, but I couldn't take offense even if I wanted to. It was the truth. Bills and ambition were the reason I'd charged him five thousand dollars for admission to the waterpark between my thighs.

"Yeah, it is," I answered, standing behind my decision.

"What bills you got that stripping don't cover?" he probed, sipping his champagne.

I sighed. "Well, if my cousin would stop blowing her money on weed and shit, maybe we wouldn't be behind on rent. And aside from household drama, I'm paying back my school loan after dropping out. Once my billing issues are straightened out, I plan to reapply."

He listened, his gaze never leaving my face. "Why'd you drop out in the first place?"

"I couldn't find the balance between school and the club. But I don't plan on dancing forever, just long enough to save enough money to pay for my way through school."

Ahsan nodded with the dip of his chin. "I respect your hustle, and like I told you Saturday night, your pussy is worth more than gold."

"So that's why you wanted to see me again? To fuck?"

"It's not the sole reason, no."

"Then what is the reason? Because nobody who looks as good as you that has your amount of money needs to spend it on something that he could willingly get for free."

"Maybe I like you."

"I thought this was a business arrangement," I clarified.

"It is."

"Then you can't like me. It's against the rules."

"I paid the money, so I make the rules."

The champagne made my mind fuzzy, and I lazily leaned into his side as the grass prickled my ankles underneath the table. His thumb traced gentle circles on my wrist.

"You make the rules, huh?"

"Yeah, I do."

"So, what are your rules on kissing?" I questioned.

I tilted my chin upward, and my eyes landed on his. *Don't get involved. Don't fall too fast or too hard. As a matter of fact, don't fall at all.* Before I could stop myself, I leaned in and pressed my lips against his. It went against every fiber in my being. But there wasn't a part of me strong enough to hold back.

Ahsan's eyes slowly opened, his seductive orbs ablaze with lust. My heart fluttered like butterfly wings brushing against my ribcage. I wanted him to fuck me like he'd never taste my pussy again. He scooped me up into his arms, and I snaked my legs around his waist before he laid me on top of the table. Ahsan gazed deep into my eyes before mashing his lips against mine, kissing as if we'd never see each other again. My body squirmed with anticipation underneath him.

He caressed my breasts through my bralette before sliding the straps down my shoulders and lowering it to my waist. He mushed my breasts together before his long tongue flicked against my hardened mounds, one by one. I watched him with intent, never wanting to miss a second. He made a trail of kisses down the center of my stomach before veering off to my inner thighs.

His breathing was slow and heavy as he worked his way toward my pussy. As a dancer, flexibility came easy to me. I held my legs wide open as he licked from the top of my clit down to the tip of my asshole. An erotic shiver inched down my spine as I tossed my head toward the ceiling and arched my back, serving up my pussy right at his soft lips. His long tongue glided up and down my smooth pussy lips like a Slip-n-Slide on a hot summer day. I looked down as Ahsan inserted his middle finger inside me. He gently sucked on my clit while looking me dead in the eyes.

"Oooh, oh my God, yes!" I cried out as waves of pleasure washed over me.

He slurped my pussy before coming up to kiss me while he buried two fingers deep inside me, pressing against my G-spot until I came.

My spine coiled as I rotated my hips around his fingers. "Ooh shiiiiit, I'm cumming!"

Ahsan bent me over the table and teased me from behind, dipping the head of his dick in and out of my warmth before plunging deep and not letting up.

"Mmm, shit," he growled, his low-cut nails digging into my hips.

He kept his hand on the top of my ass, driving me back into him. I gripped the edge of the table as he pumped fiercely. "Oh fuck!"

"You like it when I do that shit?"

I looked back at him and ran my tongue over my teeth. "Oooh, yes! It's the best dick I've ever had! Keep giving it to me!"

He picked up the pace and smacked my ass. "I'ma keep fucking you."

"That's it! Fuck this pussy!" I screamed, sucking in the air through my teeth.

After a few more back-breaking strokes, Ahsan eased out of me long enough to turn me around and pick me up. His strong arms held me suspended in the air as if I were as light as a feather. He pulled me onto the tip of his thick rod. I hooked my arms around his neck, holding on tight as he kept both arms hooked underneath my knees.

"Oooh shit, yes, Ahsan!"

"Come on, beautiful. That's it. Take this dick," Ahsan whispered in my ear while fucking me senseless.

I squealed as I tightened my ass muscles and bucked forward, creating as much pleasurable friction between our bodies as possible. He cupped my ass, thrusting deeper and deeper with the stamina of a racehorse mixed with the Energizer Bunny.

He eased me back onto the ground and returned to the doggy-style position for a few more pumps before climaxing. He placed a soft kiss on the back of my neck, panting heavily. Our private picnic was more than expensive champagne and strawberries. So much more. As good as he felt inside me and as chaotic as my thoughts and feelings were about him, I decided it was best for both of us not to risk catching any more feelings, so I planned to limit my time with him going forward. Whatever I felt for him, I needed to push it down deep.

Ahsan

ne week later.

I STEPPED INSIDE WING LEI WITH VALENTINOS ON MY FEET AND a splash of expensive cologne on my body. It was the opulent restaurant inside the luxury hotel on the Strip that Amir was holed up in while he and his girl fumbled through their on-again-off phase. I stood near the entrance, my crisp blazer and fresh white tee highlighting my broad shoulders. The aroma of jasmine tea and roasted duck clung to the air. The restaurant was bursting with vivid white, jade, and gold colors. My eyes scanned the fancy gold dining room before settling on the pomegranate trees outside the window. Amir was due at any moment. In the meantime, I pulled out my phone to text Sienna. Something about her had imprinted on me, and I couldn't shake it.

As if invited by my thoughts, she appeared. Only she wasn't

alone. She was hanging on the arm of another nigga. My breath caught. *What the fuck?* Her eyes were mixed with surprise and discomfort when she saw me staring at her. She wore a black lace bustier top with a matching satin mini skirt, dangling black earrings, and strappy black heels with curls cascading over her right eye. Her body was right, and I knew firsthand everything was soft, from her lips to her ass.

The petty nigga in me wanted to say something, but the minute I opened my mouth to speak, Amir appeared. His stride was confident, and his smile was bright and wide. He was clueless as to who she was, and I couldn't make a scene and show my ass before we'd even had a chance to eat our meals. Instead, I nodded in her direction, unable to find words before he approached.

"Sup, A?" Amir queried, greeting me with a dap-hug combo.

"Hey."

The maître d' beckoned. "Follow me to be seated."

He led us to our table. I was seething by the time we were seated. Sienna and her date were at a secluded corner table across the restaurant from us. I couldn't pry my eyes away from her. I tried to hide my obsession behind the menu decorated with gold dragons. The longer I watched her sitting with that mothafucka, the more unhinged I became. I sipped my drink while imagining caving in that nigga's kneecaps with a spiked bat.

Amir looked over his shoulder and then back at me. "You do realize you haven't stopped looking at her since we got here? You know that bitch or somethin'?"

"It's her," I confirmed.

"Who?"

"Sienna."

"Who the fuck is that?"

I sucked my teeth. "The girl I told you about from the gala."

He looked over his shoulder again. "She's bad."

"She's *mine*," I confirmed.

Amir shot me a serious look. "You got that look in your eye, nigga."

"What look?"

"The look you get when you about to fuck some shit up."

Instead of responding, I waved down the maître d' and had him send a bottle of their most expensive wine to her table. A wicked smile lifted the corner of my mouth as I watched her receive it. Her eyes frantically scanned the room in search of me, unaware I'd already set my sights on her. When her eyes finally locked on mine, I raised my glass, sending cheers to her from across the room. That should've been good enough to satisfy my thirst to be petty, but it wasn't. I wanted to do more.

I shot my eyes at Amir. "I'll be right back."

"Aw shit," he mumbled.

I strolled over to Sienna's table and stopped dead in front of her, completely ignoring the man seated across the table. "Are you enjoying my gift?" I inquired.

"This was from you?" her date asked.

"Is this a friend of yours?" I asked her.

"Sienna, who is this guy?" the man probed.

I cut him a stern glare. "Nigga, speak one more time without being spoken to, and I'll pull your mothafuckin tongue out of your fucking mouth and stab it with one of these expensive ass forks." I watched his Adam's apple bulge as he swallowed hard, eating whatever response he'd planned to say next. I turned my gaze back to Sienna. "Well? Is he?"

She slowly shook her head as her eyes blazed with disgust. She twisted her lips to the side, refusing to bless me with a response to my question. I could feel the heated rage exuding from her body. If looks could kill, we would have both been pushing up flowers.

"Are you done?" she finally asked.

I smirked. "I'm just getting started. Enjoy the rest of your night, beautiful."

I pivoted on the ball of my foot, and seconds later, I felt the not-so-gentle tap of her nails on the back of my shoulder. I halted my advance and rounded back toward her. The look on her face was unforgiving.

"Bathroom, now," she demanded.

Sienna stalked off ahead of me. I followed her toward the restrooms, where she turned to me with her arms tightly folded across her C-cup chest. The downward V of her brow was apparent, and her icy glare sliced right through me.

"You think you funny, nigga? This is my job! You embarrassed the shit out of me back there! And for what? To prove a point? How would you like it if I walked into your job and started fucking up your shit? What? You think you my pimp now? Don't get beside yourself, nigga. This is still very much my pussy!" She hissed, cussing me up and down the restaurant.

"You finished?" I quizzed, amusement laced in my tone.

She smacked her red-painted lips. "Fuck you, Ahsan!"

"Who the fuck is this cornball nigga anyway?"

"Why the fuck does it matter? Better yet, why the fuck do you care? You're not the only one in this city with green money! Stay the fuck out of my business when it doesn't concern you!"

Sienna twisted on her heels to walk away from me. I caught her swinging arm, drawing her back to me. I sucked my teeth. "Look, I'm sorry, all right?"

She kept her back turned to me as if to let me know she didn't give one fuck about anything I had to say. "It's still fuck you, nigga."

"I'm speaking to you, Sienna. Turn your gorgeous ass around." My fingertips slowly skated down her bare shoulder, causing goose-bumps to pebble up on her skin. Sienna slowly turned to face me and drew her fiery brown orbs to mine. "I'm sorry for upsetting you, but it was either that or keep sitting across the room fantasizing about bashing his skull in with a mallet when I thought about him touching you."

She scoffed. "You're not serious."

"Do you really wanna roll those dice and find out?"

Sienna eyed me closely, and I knew she peeped all the pressure I was applying. "Ahsan, you *don't* own me."

"You're not real estate, Sienna. I don't want to own you. I want to—"

"You want to what?" she barked, cutting me off as she tilted her head to the side.

I closed the gap between us as our eyes locked with an intensity that vibrated from my chest to the soles of my feet. My hand cupped her cheek, thumb brushing against her soft, sun-kissed skin. The lulled murmur of the other diners faded as I drew her lips closer to mine, magnetized by my impulsive desire to feel her. And then, in that intimate space, our lips met in a sweet collision of rage and lust. I hooked my hand around her neck while sucking on her bottom lip. The bitter taste of the expensive red wine I'd purchased lingered on her tongue. Heat pulsed between our bodies as our fingertips entwined. Our hips aligned, and our heartbeats galloped in sync like wild horses in an open field.

My lips parted from hers with slow reluctance as the sounds of the outside world came flooding back in. The clinking of dishes and forks and the distant murmur of conversations became audible again. Reality was a slow unraveling, but our connection remained tethered. My eyes bore into hers, unveiling a hunger that surpassed basic allure. Of course, Sienna was beautiful, but what I felt was deeper than face value. Everything bubbling up beneath the surface had burst through, causing me to act outside myself. I'd never kissed anyone like that before. I was caught up in a gravitational whirlpool of desire. I wanted every inch of her skin pressed against mine in a never-ending sea of entangled brown limbs.

I traced the curve of her jaw, urgency etched in my touch. "I want to get your permission to take you in that bathroom and fuck the shit out of you."

I pushed Sienna's lace panties further down into my pocket, keeping them like a trophy as I stepped away from the bathroom. I returned through the maze of tables as I approached Amir.

"Nigga," he grumbled as soon as I folded my body back into my seat.

"What?"

"I can smell the sex on you. Who the fuck is this chick that got you coming up out of yourself."

"I don't know what you're talking about," I denounced.

His brows turned downward. "You stunted on her nigga with a fifteen-hundred dollar bottle of wine. I ain't never seen you do no shit like that."

I shrugged. "So? Maybe I wanna take a page out of your book and be toxic like you."

"You be you, nigga. You could never be me," Amir said with a confident chuckle.

"Whatever, mothafucka."

"But forreal, you must feel something for her if she got you blowing money out the wazoo. What you tryna prove?"

I sighed before finally deciding to come clean about my arrangement with Sienna. "I told you we met in the bar the night of the gala. What I didn't tell you was that she's a dancer looking for a come-up, so I paid her for the night."

Amir's bushy eyebrows heightened. "A dancer? She strip?"

"Yeah."

"Hold up, nigga. Let me get this straight. You paid a stripper for pussy? Something she shows niggas for free every night?"

I cut him a stern glare. "It's deeper than that now, Amir. I wouldn't expect your shallow ass to understand."

"Yeah, I bet. No wonder your nose is wide open. You don't wanna see another nigga with his hand in the cookie jar you paid for."

"It started that way, but now, I don't know. It's more than that. She went stiff on a nigga out of nowhere, and I don't like that shit."

There wasn't a doubt in my mind Sienna was the one I wanted to be next to. I couldn't wait for my next opportunity to bless her with my dick again.

"You can stay on her ass all night if you want to, nigga. You can't turn no ho into no housewife. No matter how good the pussy is."

"Mind your tongue, nigga," I scolded him.

"Fine. All I'm saying is, save yourself now. A wet dick ain't worth the heartbreak in the end, my guy."

"I don't know. What if she is?"

"You really that lovesick over some pussy, nigga? What, you a virgin or something? That shit must have a pot of gold at the end of it because I don't know who the fuck is sitting across the table from me right now."

A hearty laugh at my expense barreled out of him. I didn't give a fuck. I was used to being the nigga in the room with the most unpopular opinion, and I was hardly ever wrong.

"Whatever, yo. You about ready to order?" I asked, trying to change the subject.

Amir pushed his menu aside and leaned in to look me square in the eye. "I bet you can't get her to fall in love with you by your birthday in a few months without waving your money around."

"And if I can?"

"You tell me. What are you brave enough to wager?"

I sat back and stroked my beard while thinking. I'd been unsure about handing over the drug business to Amir. Even though I knew he'd be great at it, I didn't want him to have to make the same sacrifices I did to stay on top. Being the HNIC left no room for unnecessary drama and distractions. With his inability to stay away from his toxic ass girl, I could see that being his downfall. He was built differently from XL and me. The nigga had no discipline when it came to his emotions.

"Fine. If I win, and I get her to fall in love with me by my thirty-fifth birthday, I'll hand over the keys to the game to the successor of my choice."

His brow creased. "Fuck you mean? Who else would you choose besides me?"

"XL," I answered.

"The fuck? XL don't want this shit like me, nigga."

"We've talked. He's had a change of mind. You and I both know he's levelheaded, which is exactly the type of nigga I need at the helm when I take my hands off the wheel for good."

Amir sucked his teeth, ready to pitch a fucking fit. "And what do I get when you lose, nigga?"

"*If* I lose, everything goes to you."

Amir shot me a devilish smirk as he extended his hand across the table for me to shake. "It's a bet then."

"Bet," I replied, firmly gripping his hand.

Truth be told, I didn't know what the fuck I'd gotten myself into. A part of me felt some type of way about doing something so childish as betting over a woman's heart, especially when I already knew she'd carved out a spot in my chest. But I wasn't the type of nigga to back down from a challenge. I would always prove I had the most brutal bite in the room, no matter who had the loudest bark. And who knew? Maybe I'd fuck around and spin the odds in my favor by telling Sienna about the bet off rip. That way, there was no deception on my part, at least not to her. Then, I could put XL in charge and free up Amir to live his life as wild and recklessly as he wanted to. Or I could play right into my brother's hand and try to win over Sienna's heart the old-fashioned way—with trial and error. Sienna had proven she was a tough cookie to crack, but something about her walled-off exterior only made me want to know her more.

My phone lit up with a text from Jules. I opened it, and my eyes scanned the screen from left to right. "Oh shit."

"What? Everything good?" Amir asked.

Instead of responding to my brother, I waved down the maître d'.

He promptly made his wave over to our table. "Send over a bottle of your finest champagne. We're celebrating tonight," I announced.

"Right away, sir," he replied before hurrying off.

Amir arched a curious brow. "Fuck are we celebrating, nigga?"

A grin spread, splitting my face from ear to ear. "The mayor accepted my proposal."

Sienna

As I stirred from my late afternoon nap, the sofa bed cradled me like a baby. I lay there for a few seconds, savoring the fleeting seconds of my drowsy haze. My phone dinged from the coffee table. I blinked a couple of times to fully wake myself up before reaching for it. The screen illuminated with a text from Ahsan, and I immediately rolled my eyes. I'd never met someone who possessed such a hold over my emotions and body. My feelings for him were split right down the middle. Half of me hated him, and the other half loved that I hated his ass.

AHSAN: *You still mad?*

I sucked my teeth, my fingers stood at the ready, but before I could type a response to his asinine question, the phone started ringing in my hand. It was him calling, too impatient to wait for my reply. I hesitated, considered tapping decline, and then answered.

His familiar yet irritating voice hit my eardrum with a low grumble. "You still mad?" he asked, his tone cautious.

I fully sat up, rubbing my eyes as a scoff escaped my lips. "Nigga, what you think?"

The memory of our last encounter lingered in the corners of my mind—a sharp exchange of words, threats, hurt feelings, and back-breaking sex. I couldn't even say it was makeup sex, but it was good, nonetheless.

"I want to see you."

"For what?"

"To talk business."

I rolled my eyes. "Business. Yeah, right. Say what you have to say, Ahsan. I'm not meeting you for dinner."

"I don't do business over the phone."

"Then that's too bad because I'm not that hungry."

"Then name the place, and I'll meet you."

I sighed. I didn't know what the fuck he wanted to talk about under the guise of a business meeting, but there was something about the rumble in his voice, a deep vulnerability I couldn't ignore.

"How about we meet at the coffee shop I go to sometimes."

"Text me the address, and I'll be there."

Again, I hesitated before agreeing. "Fine. I'll meet you there at seven. I'm texting you the address now," I said before ending the call.

My nails tapped against the screen, sending Ahsan the information for the coffee shop. My thoughts remained adrift as I walked to the bathroom to shower and get ready. After my shower and makeup routine, I smoothed my curls into a sleek low bun with a middle part and pulled out two curly strands by my ears. Then I slipped on my favorite hoop earrings, a World Series Dodgers T-shirt, sneakers, and blue cut-off jean shorts. I stepped out the front door wondering if Ahsan would reveal his true intentions at our "business meeting" and what other surprises the night would hold. If there was one thing I knew about Ahsan, there was never a dull moment with that nigga.

***

The coffee shop was slated on a busy corner. Its familiar blue-painted brick walls and vinyl signage announced its name, Mocha Brews. The fragrant scent of fresh coffee beans wafted past my nose as I stepped inside. The barista standing near the chalkboard listing the day's specials greeted me with a welcoming smile. The wooden floors creaked underneath my yellow and black Jordan one mid-tops as my eyes scanned the small space. There was no Ahsan in sight. I chose a secluded table by the window and folded my body into the seat that faced the door so I could see him when he entered. My gaze traveled across the coffee shop and saw my framed art on the wall. They'd held a contest a few years back, and I won. Perhaps one of the things I liked the most about the spot was that it showcased the work of local artists all over their establishment.

My phone lit up with a text from Diamond, interrupting my thoughts. Her words danced across the screen:

DIAMOND: *Private party this weekend. Big bank. You in?*

Shit. My fingers hovered over the keyboard, caught between two different paths. I glanced out the coffee shop's window, unsure whether to follow the money trail or avoid another public debacle with Ahsan. He'd made it clear he didn't want to see me with another man. A bit of guilt tiptoed in unannounced. Why the fuck did I care what he had to say, or better yet, how he even felt? *He's not my damn daddy. Besides, it's a private party. There's way less of a chance he'll be there. I gotta get this money.* I typed my reply.

ME: *Count me in.*

As I hit send, the coffee shop's door chimed. I glanced up, my heart fluttering with anticipation. There he stood, the man I both missed and resented. His brown orbs found mine, and a million words were said in our silent connection without our lips ever parting. Ahsan confidently approached me as if his presence was welcomed. The chair across from me scraped against the floor before he sat.

"Hey," he said, voice raw. "I'm glad you came."

"You didn't really make it seem like it was optional."

"It wasn't. I've missed your presence."

I studied him, watching his mannerisms—the way his long, brown fingers traced patterns on the table and the sincerity in his eyes. As badly as I may have wanted to cuss his ass out, being in his presence made it hard for me to stand on business.

I cleared my throat while looking over my shoulder to ensure everyone around us was out of earshot. "You still got my panties?"

"Yeah," he confirmed.

"Then take a good whiff when you get home because that's the last time you'll *ever* get close enough."

His jaw ticked as he let out an exasperated sigh. "So you are still mad."

"Didn't you get that over the phone?"

"And yet, you were here on time to meet with me."

I cut him a hard glare from across the small round table. "Whatever. Just say what you gotta say so I can get out of here."

"You got somewhere better to be?"

"That's my business, not yours."

He rolled his eyes. "Now that you've got what I hope is your last negative ass comment off your chest, can we talk business?"

"You have the floor."

He looked away while softening his tone. "I was hoping we could start over."

"And what if I don't want to?" I questioned, folding my arms across my T-shirt.

"Hear me out. I have a business proposal for you."

"I'm listening."

"I'd like to hire you."

My brow creased. "Hire me? To do what? Drive a truck?"

"I'd like to hire you to be my girl."

My eyebrows heightened. "Excuse me?"

"You need money, and I need to ensure my business ends up in the best hands possible when I step down."

"You're stepping down from your trucking business?"

"Parts of it, yes."

My heart skipped a beat. "And what does any of that have to do with me?"

"My brother was with me that night at the restaurant when you and I had our little run-in."

"And?"

"I know this is about to sound crazy but hear me out. He made me a bet I couldn't refuse. He bet me that if I made you fall in love with me by my thirty-fifth birthday, I could hand over my business to the successor of my choice which, right now, is looking like my cousin, XL."

I scoffed while wagging my head. "No. I'm cool on your offer. The gala was one thing, but this is messy, and I got enough mess in my life without adding to it."

On some levels, Ahsan's offer seemed so childish. I didn't want to get involved in something so trivial between him and his brother. But I also understood that he was looking at things from a different perspective than I was. He wanted to ensure the best outcome for his business, and if he had to fix the bet to ensure he was sure to win, he would.

"Set your price."

"Ahsan, no. I'm not doing this."

"No romantic hassles. No real feelings. It's just for a couple of months, Sienna."

"And at the end, what do I get?"

"Whatever you want," he promised.

I paused, imagining a life of financial freedom where I could do what I wanted, whenever I wanted, without having to double-check my bank account first. I could move out into my own place and buy real furniture and art supplies. As I thought more about the good, the bad started to seep in. Ahsan had already proven himself to be a charming nigga. I couldn't risk falling for a client, which was precisely what he was.

"I don't know."

Ahsan reached across the wooden table, his fingers brushing against mine. "Just think about it, all right?"

I waved him off with my free hand. "Mmhmm."

"I'm serious, Sienna. Promise me you'll think long and hard about it."

That nigga knew better than to use the words *long* and *hard* in the same sentence. My thoughts immediately went to the gutter. My emotions wavered. Once a roaring fire, my anger had been lulled into dying embers. The desire behind my anger remained. It was an ache I'd never felt before. It defied all time and logic. I studied the sincerity in his eyes and wondered if our arrangement was doable. My drawback wasn't about pretending to care. The trouble would come with pretending not to.

I huffed. "Fine. I'll think about it, Ahsan. But that's all I'm doing right now," I stated, doubling down on the fact that I didn't want to be heavily involved with a client.

"That's all I ask."

"So, we're done here?"

"For now. Let me walk you out."

"I'm a big girl, Ahsan. I can take care of myself."

"I know you can. But when you're with me, I take care of you."

"You say that like it's your job or something."

"It is. I always protect my investments."

He smirked at me, giving me a taste of my own medicine. I didn't necessarily like how it tasted. The bell on the door chimed as we exited the coffee shop. We were approaching my car when a man walking toward us on the sidewalk called out to me. "Yo, Bella? Is that you, beautiful?"

Ahsan halted in his step and looked at me. "You know this nigga?"

I quickly scanned the man from head to toe. He was a heavy-set man with shoulder-length locs and grills on his bottom teeth. "Not really. He comes to the club sometimes and asks for private dances, but he never has enough money for the VIP."

The man got closer. "Yeah, I knew that was your fine ass! When you gon' be down at the club again? I got my paper up, beautiful! I want a dance!"

Ahsan grunted, immediately losing his patience. "Nigga, you don't see me fucking standing here? You speaking to her like I'm a mothafuckin shadow. Show my girl some respect before I knock your mothafuckin teeth down your throat and pull 'em out your fucking asshole, bitch nigga," he threatened.

I put my hand on his arm. "Ahsan, it's cool. Chill, all right?"

He shoved my hand away and charged toward the man. "Ain't shit cool."

"It's fine. Just chill out, please!" I yelled at his back.

No sooner than the words fell off my lips, I blinked and caught Ahsan's fist connecting with the man's jaw. My eyes popped wide as he fell back and hit the cement with a hard thud. Ahsan stood over him, looking down at his bloodied mouth. He drew back his fist again, and I screamed.

"Ahsan, stop!"

His neck twisted toward me, and I immediately recognized the violence in his eyes. It was all too familiar. Demario used to fly off the handles like that at the drop of a dime. Sometimes, it was warranted. Most times, it wasn't. Ahsan had always given off the impression that he took no shit, but seeing it live and in color left me feeling a way. There was no listening to reason. There was no calming him down. All he saw was red. Seeing him come unhinged like that when no feelings were involved only forewarned me about the future. If he could beat a nigga bloody behind me without thinking, I knew if he fell in love with me, he'd body a nigga. That was another thing to add to the list of reasons why I didn't want to accept his offer. He reminded me too much of my past, and all money wasn't good money.

He slowly backed away from the man as if coming back into his body. "I'm sorry you had to see that," he apologized. "Are you okay?"

I scoffed. "I'm fine. He never even fucking touched me. You know what, I gotta go."

"Sienna, wait," he called out, reaching for my arm.

I stepped back, withdrawing my arm to my chest as I swung my head in a no. "I said I gotta go, Ahsan."

I hurried into my car and started the engine. He stood on the sidewalk watching me with such intent that goosebumps populated my skin. I looked in my side mirror before pulling away from the curb, my heart violently thudding in my chest. I glanced up into the rearview mirror to see him still standing there. *Fuck. What the fuck are you gonna do now, Sienna?*

---

*T*HREE DAYS LATER.

M*Y* HEELS CLICKED ACROSS THE MARBLE FLOOR OF THE HOTEL lobby as I reread my text from Diamond.

DIAMOND: *Penthouse Suite 2093*

I'd agreed to do the private party alongside Diamond, Sparkle, and a few other girls from the club. She promised big money, and from the looks of it, she was right. I'd seen nothing but money since I stepped through the hotel's entrance and knew I'd leave with a G-string full of cash. I caught my reflection in the mirrored elevator, reflecting my blush-painted lips, curly high ponytail, and sparkling mini dress. I had a change of clothes and platform heels in my bag for when it was time to dance.

The elevator dinged, and I was immediately greeted with crystal chandeliers, textured gold walls, and floor-to-ceiling windows revealing the Vegas city lights below. Around me were built-in polished stripper poles and a slew of hood niggas dripping in ice. They all had drinks in their hands as they mixed and mingled with the sea of half-naked women of all creeds and colors in the room.

With no decorations in sight, I didn't know the occasion. I wasn't even sure there was one. But it didn't seem to matter. My gaze drifted to the balcony, where a private hot tub overlooked the Strip. The water shimmered under the moonlight. As I moved deeper into the lavish suite, my eyes scanned the room, seeking familiar faces. Amidst the crowd, I spotted Diamond wearing an emerald bra and G-string with rhinestones all over them and a silk black robe. She stood by the marble fireplace, talking to a mysterious stranger leaning against the mantel. Our eyes met over his shoulder, and she smiled at me while waving me over.

"Hey," I greeted her when I approached them.

"Bella, this is Kason. He's the one behind the party. It's his birthday."

I glanced up at the man standing beside her. Our eyes locked as he smiled at me. He was tall with caramel-kissed skin. His long black locs were bleached blonde at the tips and were braided down into two French braids that stopped in the middle of his back. Tattoos were etched up and down his skin, and I could tell underneath his black T-shirt and camouflage jeans was a fit physique. One look and I could already tell he was under the influence of weed, liquor, or a combination of both. "Hi. Nice to meet you."

"Wassup, beautiful?"

Diamond shot me a mischievous smile. "He personally requested you."

"Me?"

"Yup. He says he wants you all to himself."

Kason nodded in agreement before pulling a thick wad of money out of his pocket, which caused me to smile wide. "Well, let me freshen up, and then I'm all yours."

"Bet. Come find me when you're ready, sexy."

Diamond's eyes crinkled with amusement. "Yay."

"Where are we changing?" I asked.

Diamond locked arms with me, and we slipped away. "C'mon, I'll show you."

I looked back to see his eyes following us and quickly turned around. She led me through the glittering maze of luxury, our heels tapping against the floor as we passed the DJ booth set up in the corner of the room. We walked upstairs and passed by a bedroom where I caught a glimpse of a camera on a tripod facing the bed. An eerie feeling immediately washed over me.

I leaned in and whispered, "Bitch, you didn't tell me this was a Diddy party."

She giggled. "Chill. It's not like that."

"Then what's it like?"

"So what if these niggas have their kinks? You know the kinkiest ones have the most bank."

I eased my arm out of hers as we approached a bathroom and stepped inside. "I don't know about all this, Diamond."

"Was I the only one who saw that thick ass wad of money that nigga had in his pocket downstairs for you?"

I smacked my lips. "Bitch, you know damn well I saw it."

"Then you need to fucking relax and remember the goal. You get dressed, and I'll go back downstairs to get you a drink to help you loosen up, all right? I'll be back in a few minutes."

I shook my head. Something in the milk wasn't clean, and I needed to be on all cylinders in this bitch. "Nah, I'm good. I'm not drinking tonight."

She shrugged. "Okay then. You got condoms?"

"I'm not fucking tonight either, Diamond."

Her eyes sparkled with mischief. "Okay, but just in case."

"Oh my God, get out!"

"Fine. I'll be right outside," Diamond said before closing the door behind her.

After getting dressed, my eyes traveled to the mirror, where I gazed back at my reflection. I'd painted my lips a bold crimson and had slipped into a black lace teddy that clung to my curves as if it had been painted on. I grazed over my high cheekbones and the delicate curve of my neck while adjusting my hoop earring.

"It's showtime, Bella. Time to get this money."

I exited the bathroom and walked back over to the guest of honor with Diamond close by. By then, girls were swinging around on poles, and money was flying through the air like planes in the sky.

"Hey, birthday boy. You wanna dance?" I asked with a smile.

He rubbed his palms together. "I wanna see you get wet. Let's go out to the hot tub for a little privacy," he said, sliding a fifty-dollar bill into my bra.

It wasn't the oddest request I'd ever had. "It's your world tonight. Lead the way."

He grabbed my hand and led us onto the balcony, where a few other people surrounded the hot tub nestled against the glass railing. He nodded, and they hurried inside, leaving us alone. The bubbling water shimmered under the moonlight as I slipped off my heels and dipped into the warmth. The bubbles rose around me, tickling my skin. I lifted my gaze to the night sky then down to the Strip that winded like a river of hotels and casinos. Kason folded his body into a seat right outside of the hot tub.

"You're not going to join me? The water feels so good," I said in a sultry voice while running my hands up my arms.

I tossed my head back, listening to the rumbling bass drifting from inside the suite as my body started to move to the beat. Kason began to throw the money in the water, making it rain on me.

"Chill, daddy. You getting all the money wet."

He scoffed. "You can dry it off later, bitch."

My eyes sliced through him. "I know it's your birthday, and you're a lil faded, but no need for the disrespect, all right?"

He tossed his hands up in surrender. "My fault, beautiful. I'll chill."

"Thank you."

The DJ started spinning Juvenile's "Rodeo" as I eased down one of my bra straps and started squeezing my tassel-covered nipples and rubbing on my breasts through my teddy. Kason's eyes were trained on me, hypnotized by how I moved my body. I continued to tease him through dance while inching down the other strap. I continued to slide the wet lace down my hips before tossing it at his feet. He leaned down and picked it up before crinkling it up with his fists.

"Now come here and shake that sexy ass on a nigga."

I pulled myself out of the hot tub and started dancing on him upon request with just my G-string and tassels on. He started getting handsy, trying to squeeze on my breasts or slip his grabby hands between my thighs. I stopped him once; minutes later, he pressed his luck again.

I swatted his hand away before getting up. "Nigga, chill out before I fucking stop!" I warned.

"C'mon, don't be like that. It's my birthday, remember? Let me see that pussy before I bend you over and slide a Benjamin down the crack of your ass."

My brow creased at the zooted, dreaded monster. "I'm not into all that, all right?"

Kason frowned before waving the money in my face. "This stack says otherwise. Now bend that ass over so I can fuck you over this balcony," he said before unbuckling his jeans.

"Nigga, I don't care how much money you have, I'm not fucking you."

Before I could react, his crazy ass had put his hand around my neck and tried to choke me out over the balcony. My mouth gaped open in an attempt to scream for help, and he stuffed my balled-up teddy into my mouth to keep me muted. My lungs clung to the last gulp of air as my nails clawed at his strong, tatted hands. He pinched my throat so tight it felt like I was holding my breath underwater.

My vision blurred, and my heartbeat rang in my ears, urging me to draw breath. Kason pressed against my chest, a harsh reminder of his power over me. The tightness of his grip increased, compressing my lungs and ribcage. My feet left the ground, suspended in a momentary levitation. It was a weightlessness that defied gravity as if my soul was preparing to leave my body.

Kason let go, dropping me back to my feet. I fell to my knees, coughing out the lace and gasping for fresh air. Without looking back,

I ran straight out of there and back inside. After racing back upstairs to grab my things, I pulled out my car keys and headed downstairs for the elevator. Each second became more precious as I waited for the doors to open. Kason made it clear that I was expendable in the eyes of niggas like him, and I had to get the fuck out of there.

My heart thundered in my chest as my thoughts swirled like twigs caught in a tornado. I *never* wanted to be in another position like I was at that party. I swore I'd never do another private party with Diamond's ass again. I didn't want to believe she'd set me up, but I'd be lying if I said the thought didn't cross my mind.

I thought back to Ahsan's offer and how he said he'd give me whatever amount I wanted. That money would give me the security I needed to stop dancing and finally focus one hundred percent on my art and getting back into school. Until now, I'd stood firm in my decision to decline Ahsan. After seeing him fuck up that man in public with one hit, I knew I was doing us both a favor. Yet, after everything that happened at the party, he was the only person I wanted to call. He may have been possessive, but he made me feel safe. I knew nothing bad would ever happen to me in Ahsan's presence. Before I knew it, my phone was pressed to his ear, waiting for him to pick up.

"Sienna?" He answered as if shocked to see me calling him.

I sniffled. "Yeah. It's me."

"You okay?"

Those two words held so much weight that tears welled in my eyes the second I heard them. "I honestly don't know."

"What do you mean you don't know? What's wrong?"

"I-I went to this private party to dance, and everything was fine at the beginning, but then things started getting weird with the birthday boy, and—"

Ahsan cut me off. "Did he hurt you?"

My hand immediately found my throat. I could still feel his grip around it. "He tried to, but I'm okay."

"Where are you? I'm coming to get you."

"No. I'm not telling you that."

"Why the fuck not?"

"Because I don't want you to fuck around and kill somebody, Ahsan! It's not worth it."

"You are!"

I sighed. "Ahsan, I'm not telling you where I am. It doesn't matter anymore, anyway. I left. I'm on my way home now."

"Fine. I'll meet you at your place. I'm leaving now," he declared before ending the call.

Ahsan

I sped through the city streets. My heart pounded, each beat urging me closer to Sienna. Our phone call had been brief, but I'd heard the tremor in her voice that told me something wasn't right, no matter what her mouth said. Twenty minutes later, I was standing outside her apartment door. My knuckles collided against it with a frantic rhythm. The hallway light flickered above me, casting shadows on the chipped paint.

The door opened, and my breath caught. Sienna's cousin, Zyon, stood there, her eyes wide with surprise. Her hair was pulled back in a messy bun, and she wore a faded Black Panther T-shirt. We'd never met in person, but Sienna had mentioned her in conversation.

"Can I help you?" she asked, her voice blurring with curiosity and concern.

I didn't waste time with pleasantries. "Is Sienna here?"

"Nigga, who the fuck are you, and what are you doing here asking for my cousin?"

"Where's Sienna?"

"I'ma ask you one more time who you are before I call the cops."

"I'm Ahsan. She knows exactly who I am."

"She might, but I don't."

"Look, I just need to make sure she's okay."

"Wait here," she said before slamming the door in my face. She returned a few minutes later, unlocked the chain on the door, and stepped aside. "She's in the bathroom taking a shower. She said you can go in."

I quickly pushed past her, my heart pounding. The apartment smelled of lavender and Black Love incense. I followed the sound of running water, my footsteps creaking underneath the floor. The bathroom door was ajar, steam billowing out like smoke.

I knocked softly. "Sienna?"

No answer. I gently pushed the door open. Sienna stood there, her silhouette hidden behind the shower curtain. Water droplets clung to her skin, forging paths down her caramel curves. Her eyes widened when she saw me, shock and happiness mingling.

"Ahsan?" Sienna's voice was as soft and fragile as a whisper.

I stepped closer, ignoring the water on the floor. "What happened, Sienna? Why did you sound so scared on the phone?"

She hesitated then pulled back the curtain after shutting off the shower. Her melanated face was flushed, and mascara-streaked tear tracks mixed with the water on her cheeks. Her fingers trembled as she reached for the towel hanging on the back of the door.

Her haunted gaze met mine. "I went to dance at a private party tonight at a hotel, and one of the guys there, it was his birthday. He got a little out of control."

My fists balled up, trying to contain my rage. "Out of control, how?" Before she fixed her lips to reply, my eyes scanned her body from head to toe. I frowned when I noticed the dark marks around her neck. "Sienna, did that mothafucka put his hands on you?"

"He was drunk, and he tried t-to..."

"Tell me," I demanded, my voice low and steady.

She met my gaze, sadness etched in her eyes. "He choked me out over the balcony because I wouldn't fuck him! I was fucking terrified.

All I could see was this blurry image of his dreads swinging in my face."

My blood boiled with rage. "Did that mothafucka force himself on you?"

Sienna sat perched on the edge of the toilet seat, her wet strands curling at the ends. I knelt before her, our knees almost touching. "All he did was choke me and shove my lingerie in my mouth. Nothing else happened, I swear. Once he let me go, I got my shit, and I got the fuck out of there without taking a dime. All I cared about was my fucking life."

I reached for her hand, intertwining our fingers. "And how do you feel now?"

"I'm still shaken up, but I'm okay."

"Good. Now tell me what his fucking name was and what hotel you were at," I demanded, bombarding her with questions before I went to personally put a nigga in his place.

"No. I said I'm okay now, Ahsan. I'm serious. I didn't call you for that. I don't want any retaliation on my behalf."

"Then why the fuck did you call me if you didn't want me to fucking handle it?" I barked, ready to smack fire from a nigga.

"I called because I-I thought about your offer."

"And?"

"You said if you win, you get to choose the successor of your business, right?"

"Yeah."

"Listen, I don't want to be in another situation like I was tonight. It made me realize how lucky I am to have the security at the club and people like you when shit gets hectic. So, if you win, I want enough money to attend art school. I want a full ride."

"Which is how much?"

"About thirteen thousand per year."

I leaned forward, studying her face. "Is that all you require?"

"No."

"What else?"

"We need to set some ground rules."

"Such as?"

"Let me throw on some clothes first. I'll meet you in the living room."

The small living room enveloped me as I sat on the couch near the lamp. Sienna walked in and sat down beside me, ready to establish a set of unspoken rules for our fake relationship to ensure our ruse remained believable.

Sienna began. "In the coffee shop, you said no romantic hassles, right? So I just want to be sure that we're still on the same page with no emotional attachment. Whatever relationship we have is purely for show."

I dipped my chin. "Done. But we have to look and act like a couple, which means knowing small shit like each other's likes and dislikes. Any awkwardness in how we interact with one another in public could raise suspicion, especially around my brother. Something tells me he'll be looking for us to slip up."

"That's fair. And behind closed doors?"

"We can drop the act."

"Okay."

"This goes without saying, but no outside relations. You already know I'm capable of causing bodily harm to a nigga."

"Right. Anything else?"

"No. You?"

Sienna shrugged her shoulders. "I guess I should let you know I hang up on niggas, and I don't hold hands."

I chuckled. "Noted. So, do we have a deal?" I asked, outstretching my hand to seal the deal with a handshake.

She agreed with a quick nod. "Yeah. We have a deal."

"Bet. I'll have my assistant handle the payment. Half now, and the other half after my birthday."

"Seriously?"

"Yeah. Send me the routing and account number where you want the money deposited."

"Can I ask you something?" she quizzed, tilting her head to the left.

"Shoot."

"Why me?"

"Why not you?"

She sucked her teeth. "I'm being serious. You could've chosen anyone."

"Because I can tell you're genuine," I said. "And because I've seen the way you look at those unfinished canvases over there. It's the same way I feel about my business. It's the passion. You can't fake that shit."

Sienna kept her head to the side, considering my answer. "You sure there's nothing else in it for you besides winning the bet?"

"Nothing unless you know something I don't."

"No. I was just curious."

I dipped my chin, wondering if the rules we'd set in place would be enough to shield our hearts from the unexpected.

I SAT QUIETLY ON THE COUCH WITH SIENNA FOR THE NEXT couple of hours, gently stroking her curls as she drifted off to sleep. I listened to her steady breathing until I was sure she was sound asleep. Then I reached for her phone and gently pressed her thumb to the screen to unlock it. I scrolled to her messages, the last one being from someone named Diamond.

DIAMOND: *Penthouse Suite 2093*

Carefully, I sent the penthouse number to myself before locking her phone. I eased my lap from underneath her head, making sure not to wake her. My hand extended toward the coffee table to grab my keys when the kitchen light flipped on. I turned to see Sienna's cousin walking toward the refrigerator.

"Hey," I whispered, slowly approaching her. "Sorry about our initial interaction earlier. I'm Ahsan. It's nice to meet you."

She looked me up and down. "Zyon."

"Do you know where Sienna was tonight? She mentioned something about a party at a hotel."

She looked up from the fridge, slightly surprised. "Oh, yeah, she was at a party at Caesar's Palace. Why?"

I shot her a sly smile and nodded. "Just curious. Thanks, Zyon. She's sleep, so I'ma head out."

"Night."

"Night."

I quietly left the apartment, making sure to gently close the door behind me. As I stepped into the night air, I pulled out my phone and called Amir. He answered on the third ring. "Hello?"

"Send a message to our hittas, nigga. We need to pay somebody a visit," I grumbled, getting into my car, starting the engine and driving off.

Two days later.

Sienna and I met for an early lunch at a cozy café downtown. The fragrance of roasted coffee beans and toasted, yeasty bagels filled the air. The café was a mix of rustic and modern decor with exposed brick walls and polished hardwood floors. A row of booths lined one side, their tables decorated with faux succulents with pendant lights hanging overhead.

I sat across from Sienna dressed in a crisp white tee, dark jeans, and a gold watch and Cuban link chain. I watched the sunlight cast a gentle glow across her beautiful face. She was clad in a vibrant sundress that swept across the floor, oversized sunglasses, and a colorful headwrap. Her nails tapped rhythmically on the table as if she were playing invisible piano keys.

"Let's play Twenty-One Questions," she suggested. "We'll take turns asking each other anything. It can be deep, silly, mysterious, whatever. No holding back, all right? And it's gotta be the truth."

I dipped my chin. "Bet. Sounds like a challenge. You go first."

"All right. If you could have any superpower, what would it be?"

"Easy. Teleportation. Imagine being able to be wherever you wanted to be whenever you wanted to be there. You?"

"Invisibility. I'm robbing a bank immediately. I'm talking big face hunnids." She giggled while imitating Plies.

I laughed. "If you could paint something for me right now, what colors would you use?"

Sienna paused, studying my eyes for a few silent seconds. I stared back, watching her mysterious eyes sparkle. "Bold blues for your laughter and warm oranges for your aspirations. Maybe specks of gold for class."

A smile lifted one side of my mouth. I admired her passion for art and her drive to flex her creative muscle whenever she wanted to. "Dope."

"What about you?" Sienna questioned. "Any hidden talents?"

"You mean besides my dancing?" I boasted.

She giggled, remembering how I spun her ass around the dance floor the first time we met. "How'd you learn to dance anyway?"

"Big Mama taught me to dance in the living room. I'm talking about old school Motown records playing on blast, laughter, cussing when I stepped on her toes, and all that." I reminisced with a chuckle.

Talking about her had pinged the soft spot I still had. She'd still been holding on through life support, and her latest scans hadn't been any better than the ones prior. I wagged my head, clearing my mind of those thoughts to focus on the present.

"Wow. I low-key love that. Most niggas say their grandmothers taught them how to cook, not dance."

"Well, I can't cook to save my ass. That's all my cousin XL. Over here, takeout is a nigga's culinary savior. Big Mama taught us all something different. It was dancing with me, cooking with XL, and money with my brother Amir."

"I like that, churning out strong, independent men."

"What about you? Can you burn in the kitchen?"

A soft giggle slipped past her lips. "I've *burned* more than one batch of cookies in my lifetime, but I can do a couple of things. I got a few staple meals locked and loaded in the chamber," she boasted.

"Yeah? Like what?"

"Spaghetti, tacos, biscuits and gravy, pancakes."

"Mmm. I used to love waking up to Big Mama's pancakes on Sunday mornings. The smell of fresh maple syrup and butter cracking in the pan felt like home."

She smiled. "That's wassup."

"Speaking of food, are you hungry? The waitress keeps circling our table like a vulture."

"No. I'm just enjoying our conversation, if I'm being honest. I'm not really that hungry."

"Me neither."

"Maybe we could order something light?" she suggested, eyes scanning the menu. "Mmm. I love chocolate cake. It's my weakness. You wanna split a piece?"

"Bet."

Neither of us were overly hungry but agreed to split a slice of rich chocolate cake down the middle. When it arrived, Sienna's eyes widened as I dipped my fork into the frosting and fed her a bite. The sweetness lingered on her lips before she licked it off, and I realized this woman, with her gentle gestures, was someone I wanted to explore further, bet or not.

I kicked off our game of questions again. "Tell me more about your family. I met your cousin the other night, but what about your childhood? What's your favorite childhood memory?"

"Summers with my cousins back in Miami used to be lit growing up. We always thought we were grown, grown. Fake IDs in the club, trying to become famous."

"You still wanna be famous?"

She shrugged. "In a different way now. I want to be famous for my art, something that will live on long after me."

"Your legacy."

Sienna nodded with a ghost of a smile. "Yeah."

"That's wassup. Okay, next question. If you could time travel, where would you go?"

She leaned back in her seat while tapping her chin as if she were in deep thought. "Hmm. I think I'd have to say the Harlem Renaissance. I can't imagine the dopeness I'd paint if I were a part of such a dope, creative era. Now, what's your guilty pleasure song? I'm talking about the song you play when no one's around, and you can blast that shit as loud as you want," she probed with a curious brow.

"Easy. 'Purple Rain' by Prince. It's a mothafuckin masterpiece," I said unapologetically. "Yours?"

"Don't judge me."

"No judgment here."

"It's 'No Scrubs' by TLC. I know Left Eye's verse forward and backward."

I chuckled. "And your favorite color?"

"Turquoise. Yours?"

"Black."

"Why black?" Sienna quizzed.

"Because it symbolizes the depths of the darkness, power, luxury, and class, everything I embody."

"Agreed. All right, my turn. What would your dream destination be if you could go anywhere right now?"

I leaned forward. "Hmm, that's a tough one. I've always been drawn to the islands. Put me on a plane destined for somewhere in the Caribbean, and I'm sure I'll find myself right at home."

Sienna's hand lurched toward the plate to take the final bite of cake and accidentally knocked over the saltshaker. I reached across the table to steady it.

"Oh shit!" She squealed. "My bad."

We both laughed. "On a scale from one to ten, how clumsy are you?" I teased.

Sienna playfully rolled her eyes, her fanned lashes fluttering toward the sky. "Shut up, bighead! It was an accident."

As the chocolate cake crumbs settled, we leaned back in our chairs. The sun had shifted downward, casting a warm glow across the wooden table as I paid the bill, and we stood to leave. I held the door open for Sienna like a true gentleman. I slipped my hand into hers. Her hand, adorned with colorful rings to match her dress, hesitated for a heartbeat before intertwining with mine. She didn't pull away as we walked side by side, steps easily falling into sync.

I looked down at her. "Thought you didn't hold hands," I noted while watching the golden sun rays wash over the sidewalk.

"I'm doing a lot of things I said I wouldn't do nowadays."

"Is that a good thing or a bad thing?"

Sienna smirked. "Ask me again on your birthday when all this is over."

"Speaking of my birthday, the mayor accepted my proposal."

"And what exactly was it about? You didn't go into much detail at the gala, and we were practically strangers, so I wasn't going to press you about it."

"I want to purchase and develop some land with a mix of luxury real estate, affordable housing, and black-owned businesses. I'd even like to have a community center where local youth can explore art or music, even dancing or science, and shit, whatever they want. I want it to be a safe space for creativity in the community, and if it keeps lil niggas off the streets, well, that's a win-win."

Sienna smiled. "I think that's beautiful, Ahsan. I can already see the kids creating some dope ass colorful murals on the walls, inside and out."

Her smile made my lips spread into one, too, as she pointed out a small graffiti mural on the side of a building we were approaching. It was a mix of vibrant colors spray painted over red bricks.

"Something like this would be dope," I agreed.

I gazed at Sienna as if she were the only woman on Earth I had eyes for. My eyes had a blend of curiosity and awe while tracing the delicate contours of her face, from the curve of her lips to the sparse freckles on her cheeks. She was a masterpiece.

We passed by a street musician playing a soulful tune on his bongo drums. I halted my slide, fishing around inside my wallet for a few dollars. Sienna watched in silence. I could see her heart swelling behind her gaze. It was as if our souls recognized each other after being apart for decades, and we were finally catching up on all the time we'd missed.

We continued our stroll through the streets, continuously peeling back the layers of our lives to each other to get more acquainted. We didn't know everything about each other yet, but the information I had learned about her was vital. I got to see beyond the woman with the stack of unfinished canvases in her living room. The city buzzed around us, but at that moment, we were simply Ahsan and Sienna, learning each other's ins and outs, one quirk at a time.

Sienna

One week later.

THE HOT SUMMER AIR ENVELOPED AHSAN AND ME AS WE walked the mini golf course, finding bits of shade under the palm trees. I wore a white minidress with my favorite sunglasses and sneakers as I surveyed the windmill ahead. Ahsan stood beside me, his muscular arms casually folded.

"Your turn," he said, gesturing toward the slow-churning windmill.

I stepped forward, my fingers brushing against his as he handed me the putter. I drew my arms back and swung it, sending the ball soaring through the rotating blades. It popped out on the other side and rolled toward the hole.

"Nice shot. You're a dangerous woman," Ahsan complimented, squinting his eyes toward the sun.

He followed suit, aiming for the loop-de-loop. His ball circled the cup before plunking inside. I clapped for him as a giggle slipped past my lips. I didn't know why I was so giddy. Our competitive nature only intensified as we followed the path, moving from one hole to the next. Ahsan took his time stepping up for this turn. Instead of swinging right away, he pretended to study the slope of the green with a serious expression.

"Boy! If you don't go ahead and swing!" I called out to his back with a laugh.

My laughter must have been contagious because he started laughing too. I studied how his deep-set eyes crinkled whenever he smiled, each laugh cracking through his hard exterior. I was curious about what secrets lay hidden behind his guarded eyes.

He finally swung and landed another perfect shot. "That's almost game, baby!" Ahsan bragged.

"Winner buys ice cream," I declared, playfully nudging him. I hesitated when we reached the water hazard—a pond between the ground and the hole. "I've never been good at these," I confessed. "But I guess I'll give it a shot."

"Better not chicken out now," Ahsan teased, stepping behind me. His firm, steady hands guided mine on the putter. "Guess I'll lend a hand," he whispered.

We swung in unison, watching the ball skim over the top of the water before landing on the small island in the center. My laughter bubbled up through my throat. "Ahh!"

Ahsan kissed my temple.

"Teamwork makes the dream work," he said, his voice low and intimate as he spun me around in his arms.

I leaned in, my lips brushing against his. "Always."

But just as we prepared for the final hole, Ahsan's phone buzzed in his pocket. He frowned after glancing at the screen. "Hold up a second. It's my brother," he announced apologetically.

He pressed his phone to his ear, and I watched his entire demeanor change in the blink of an eye. His arm fell limp before he pulled the phone away from his ear and looked at me without saying anything.

"What's wrong?" I questioned.

"We gotta go."

My heart skipped a beat as my concern mirrored his. "Ahsan, what happened?"

"It's Big Mama."

"Oh my God, okay. Yes! Let's go!"

Ahsan and I dropped our golf clubs where we stood and hurried out of the establishment. He sped toward the hospital while I silently held down the passenger seat. I didn't know what to say. All I could do was be there.

AHSAN AND I SPRINTED ACROSS THE HOSPITAL PARKING LOT. My breath came in ragged gasps, and my heart thudded against my ribcage. I could only imagine the thoughts going through his head. We burst through the metal elevator doors, Ahsan's eyes frantically scanning the corridor of the ICU wing. He raced toward two men standing near the nurse's station. Their faces were both etched with grief.

"What happened to Big Mama? Is she okay?" Ahsan questioned.

The man who looked similar to him swung his head in a low dip, his eyes red-rimmed. "She had two back-to-back seizures. She's gone, bro."

"What? Gone? Why the fuck wasn't I called?"

The other man's voice cracked as he approached. "The doctor said it all happened so fast. They tried everything they could to save her, but she was gone."

Ahsan's legs turned to jelly, and he leaned against the nearest wall for support. I quickly raced to his side, feeling the thickness of grief in the air. Their grandmother, the head of their family who had raised them as her own sons, was gone.

His cousin stepped forward and rested his hand on Ahsan's shoulder. "She fought hard, bro. But it was her time."

Ahsan nodded, unable to find words.

"I'm sorry for your loss," I said, making eye contact with them all before tearing my gaze to the ground.

His brother's brow creased. "Who the fuck are you, and why the fuck are you here right now?"

Ahsan jumped in before I had the chance to. "Chill, nigga. She's good. She's with me."

He scoffed. "So you're the one my brother's been spending all his free time with."

"My name is Sienna," I asserted, unafraid to speak up for myself.

"Amir," he replied. "And you said you met my brother where?"

"We met at the gala a few weeks back."

"Hmm. A few weeks, and you're already dipping your nose in family business?"

"I didn't mean any disrespect by showing up. Your brother and I were on a date when he got the call. We dropped everything and came straight here."

Ahsan grunted while running his hand down his beard. "I said she's good."

"She shouldn't be here," Amir protested. "This is family business, like I said."

"Both of y'all niggas, chill. It doesn't matter who else is here as long as we're together. Let's go see her," his cousin encouraged, guiding Ahsan down the sterile hallway.

The fluorescent lights flickered overhead, casting a ghostly glow on the sneaker-streaked floor. We passed by nurses, their faces solemn with condolence as we approached the room where their grandmother's body lay.

"I'll wait out here," I suggested.

Amir's expression darkened as he crossed his arms, blocking my path. "Yeah. You fuckin' do that," he snapped.

I cringed, taken aback by his hostile ass attitude. I understood grief took on many forms, but he'd been at my throat since the moment I showed up at Ahsan's side.

"Look, I'm just here to be with Ahsan. He needs support, just like you."

Amir's eyes narrowed. "Is your last name Patton? You think you're part of this family now because you're fucking, excuse me, I mean *dating* my brother?"

Ahsan stepped between us, his grief still visibly raw. "Amir, don't make me have to put you in one of these hospital beds, nigga. She's important enough to me to be here. End of fucking story," he barked, yoking his brother up by his collar.

Amir scoffed, shoving him off. "Big Mama is gone, nigga! And you're wasting your time with some ho you barely know?"

My cheeks flushed, but I refused to let his rude ass knock me off my square. "I care about Ahsan because he's my man! And because you're an extension of my man, I have to care about you, too, to some extent. So again, I'm sorry for your loss. But don't get shit twisted, nigga. Watch your fuckin' mouth when you speak to me or about me!"

XL, who had been standing by like a silent shadow, stepped forward. "Enough, Amir. We're all hurting. Stop making shit worse!"

Ahsan grabbed my hand, his voice firm. "Like I said, she stays."

Amir's jaw clenched, but he stepped back, allowing me to approach the door. The small hospital room was a sterile space where the intersections of life and loss met. My gaze shifted to the hospital bed, where their grandmother lay still. Tubes and monitors surrounded her. The silent machines no longer needed to monitor her fragile existence. Ahsan approached the bed and reached for her hand, his fingers brushing against her cold skin as a tear streamed down his cheek.

"Rest now, Big Mama," he whispered. "You've earned your peace."

The four of us stood together in silence, united by grief. I stepped out of the room, my eyes puffy from the emotional roller coaster. I needed a moment to collect myself and give Ahsan a minute alone to say his final goodbyes. The hallway felt quieter, giving me more space and time to collect my thoughts.

As I leaned against the wall, Amir emerged from the room, his expression softer than before. He cleared his throat, avoiding direct eye contact. "It's Sienna, right?" he asked. "I owe you an apology for how I came at you earlier."

Surprised by his sudden change of heart, I raised an eyebrow but agreed to blame it on the grief. "I understand."

He shifted his weight from one foot to the other. "I may be the baby, but I'm protective over my family. Seeing you here threw me off, that's all. But I can see you care about him in a way I haven't seen before."

I folded my arms across my chest while studying him. "And that bothers you?"

"It does if it's not real."

"What do you mean by that?" I asked as the bet came to the front of my mind.

"I'm just having a hard time believing that your bond has grown so tight in such a short time."

I shifted my weight, leaning against the hallway wall. His curiosity was understandable—after all, Ahsan and I had only known each other for a few weeks, but those weeks had been filled with the most laughter and fun I'd had in years.

"We met at the gala," I said, a smile tugging at my lips.

Amir raised a suspicious brow. "He told me he paid you that night."

"And? That was then, and this is now."

"Did my brother put you up to this?"

I frowned. "What? No."

"Seriously. Is he paying you to be here right now? You can tell me."

"Amir, I don't know what you're talking about. He's not paying—"

He cut me off with his own wager. "I'll double whatever he's offering you."

I cocked my head to the left. "You seem to have already made up your mind about me, and that's fine. I don't give a fuck. But your brother deserves happiness, and if I provide him with that, you need to take a look within yourself and figure out why that's so hard for you to accept. Because that's your problem, not ours."

He sighed. "I'm sorry, yo. I guess losing Big Mama made me realize how fragile life is."

My gaze softened. "I'm not here to replace you or anyone else. Like I said earlier, I just want to be here for your brother."

He finally met my gaze, his eyes glassy. "I know. And maybe it's time I let go of my protective instincts. I guess you seem good for him."

I nodded. "Thank you. I think he's good for me too. We're still feeling things out, but I'm really happy."

Amir nodded, his stern expression softening. "Take care of him," he said.

I touched my heart. "Always," I promised. "Ahsan is lucky to have you as a brother."

He glanced back at the hospital room, where Ahsan and XL stood by their grandmother's bedside. "He needs someone like you," he said, "someone who cares and ain't afraid to go toe-to-toe with a nigga and hold your own. I respect it." He extended his hand to dap me up.

Our hands collided with a cool slap as we forged an unspoken truce in the quiet hospital hallway. Suddenly, Ahsan emerged from the room. I observed Ahsan's dark eyes lingering on us a little too long and knew he wanted to know what we were discussing.

A cocktail of conflicting emotions swirled around in the pit of my stomach. No matter how badly I told myself it was all about the money and my chance to attend art school without worrying about the financial burden, I could feel something shift within me every time I was in Ahsan's presence. The stolen kisses felt less staged, the dates more fun and romantic, and I'd even become accustomed to the hand-holding. Beneath the pretense, I wondered if there was a chance for a real connection that surpassed the bet he'd made with his brother.

He approached us. "Everything good?"

Amir dipped his chin. "Yup."

I nodded. "Yeah. We're good."

"You ready to go?" Ahsan queried.

I nodded before willingly slipping my hand in his. "Yeah. Let's go."

<hr>

WE WERE A FEW MINUTES AWAY FROM MY APARTMENT WHEN I reached out and pulled his hand into my lap. "I just want you to know you're not alone in this, Ahsan," I muttered, my voice soft. "I truly am sorry to hear about your grandmother."

My approach was gentle and reassuring. I knew that words alone couldn't mend the ache piercing Ahsan's heart, but I at least hoped my presence would provide him with solace. Instead of responding verbally, he glanced at me and squeezed my hand. I studied the lines of fatigue framing his sorrowful eyes. He refocused them on the road ahead and continued to drive.

"I can't believe she's fucking gone," he choked out.

I unhooked my seat belt and swallowed him up with my embrace, pulling him into a tight hold after he pulled into the nearest parking spot. "It's okay to grieve," I muttered. "Let it out. It's just us here."

I pressed a kiss to his forehead, a silent promise to weather the storm beside him as I held his body to mine. He leaned into my embrace, his warmth enveloping me. For a moment, he allowed himself to be vulnerable.

"Thanks," he whispered. "I haven't figured out how to live without her."

I stroked the back of his head, my touch soothing. "You don't have to. We'll figure it out day by day together."

Suddenly, a wave of doubt washed over me. There was no one around but us. Was it really all an act? Or did we both feel something real maturing beneath the surface? *I can't risk my heart becoming even more entangled in our charade than it already is, can I?*

Ahsan

I sat behind my mahogany desk, feeling the weight of the world pressing down on my shoulders. I'd spent the week planning Big Mama's homegoing service. Jules had been relaying messages from the funeral director all hours of the day and night. Between that and moving forward with the next phase of my business plan with the mayor, my trucking business was thriving, but so were my headaches. I just wanted it all to be over.

I massaged the back of my neck, feeling the knots of stress beneath my fingertips. Jules stood by the door. She'd seen me through countless crises, from late shipments to financial audits.

"Ahsan," she said, her voice steady, "I say this with all due respect, but you look like shit. You need to take a break. Go home early and take some time off before and after the funeral. Hell, get a massage."

My eyes flickered. "A massage?" I repeated, surprised.

"Why not? It's a masseuse's job to destress you."

"That actually sounds like just what I need."

Jules's full lips curved into a knowing smile. "Say less. I'll hit up my masseuse and book one for you. And maybe, for someone else too?" she asked with hesitance.

I looked up and caught her gaze pinned on me. I leaned back in my leather chair, considering. Of course, Sienna was the first person to come to mind. I'd been so wrapped up in the funeral arrangements we hadn't seen much of each other since the night at the hospital.

"Good thinking. Book a couple's massage for me and Sienna."

She choked on her spit. "I'm sorry, who?"

"Sienna. The woman I told you about from the gala."

"I wasn't aware you were still seeing her."

"Yeah. I am."

"Is it serious?" she probed.

I had Jules wire the first half of Sienna's payment to her under the guise of a scholarship fund. I didn't need or want extra people in our business, and I knew she would appreciate the confidentiality.

"It's getting there."

Her brows heightened. "Wow."

"Wow? That's all you got to say?"

"I mean, I'm shocked, Ahsan. You've been Mr. Anti-Cupid since I've known you, and all of a sudden, it's like you've been bitten in the ass by the lovebug. It's a different look on you."

"What? Happiness?"

After my request, I sensed the subtle shift in her demeanor—the brooding glare whenever I mentioned Sienna's name, or her voice heightening whenever she asked questions about her.

She cocked her head to the side with a subtle curiosity in her eyes. "So that's what that look is? Happiness?"

There was a twinge of jealousy in her voice. It wasn't overly noticeable, but who knew what secrets she'd kept behind her composed exterior. I'd always been too busy, focused on the weight of my responsibilities pulling me deeper into the weeds of my empire. And with Sienna now in my corner, I had no desire to look at or talk to another female in that way.

Before stepping into the shower, I texted Sienna to let her know I needed her to clear her schedule for me. I planned to pick her up within the hour and told her to wear something comfortable. The sound of cascading water filled the bathroom as I closed the shower door behind me, letting the warm water wash over me. I scrubbed my body from head to toe, thinking about the day ahead. I had Jules set up a full spa day for Sienna and me and couldn't wait to surprise her.

After my shower, I trekked into my spacious closet with my towel around my waist. I browsed through my collection of clothes before settling on a soft cotton white T-shirt and gray joggers. I completed my look with my gold chain and brushed down my waves before heading out the door. Before long, I was sliding into the driver's seat of my car, feeling the warm leather against my skin as I started the engine.

On the way to Sienna's place, I had my GPS find the nearest flower shop. I sailed inside and returned to my car moments later with a fresh bouquet of rich red roses. I was still trying to navigate through the fog of losing Big Mama. Her absence resonated with me more than ever. Yet, I found myself reaching out to Sienna with romantic gestures, almost instinctively. It was strange how both grief and love had found a way to coexist inside me.

It was almost as if each kind act I showed her was in some way a tribute to Big Mama. I knew she would've liked Sienna if given the chance. She would've told me to hold onto her tight. Since Big Mama's death, Sienna had been a daily reminder that there could be beauty amid my sorrow.

Fifteen minutes later, my car glided to a slow crawl outside her apartment building. I glanced at the passenger seat, checking the roses one last time and adjusting my chain around my T-shirt collar before stepping out. I headed for her apartment with the roses and confidence in my step. As soon as the door opened, I handed them to her with a gentle smile. She didn't know it, but her presence helped me find peace, even in fragments.

Sienna's eyes lit up at the sight of the roses. "Thank you. They're beautiful, but what's the occasion?"

"Do I need a reason?"

She playfully rolled her eyes. "You're too much. You know that, don't you? Let me put these in water, and then I'll be ready."

We made our way back to the car and got inside. The interior was still filled with the floral aroma of her roses. As she buckled up, I reached into my glove compartment and pulled out a red silk blindfold.

I cleared my throat. "I've got one more surprise for you, Sienna. Close your eyes and put this on."

She glanced at me, curiosity sparking in her brown eyes. "A blindfold? Really? You and your surprises." She giggled. "Where are you taking me, Ahsan? You know I hate not knowing."

"Just trust me," I replied. "It will be worth it."

She smirked before tying the blindfold over her eyes. "Fine, I'll play along."

The car engine hummed to life, and I drove off. I let the anticipation build until I brought the car to a complete stop. I guided her out, leading her from the passenger seat to the front of the spa before removing the blindfold.

She opened her eyes and blinked, speechless. "We're going to the spa?"

"Full spa day on me," I announced, excited to treat her to the finer things in life.

"Are you sure about this? A whole day?"

I nodded. "Absolutely. We've both been working tirelessly. It's time for us to unwind."

"This is the nicest thing anybody has ever done for me," she admitted.

"You deserve it."

We stepped inside. The air was filled with the calming scents of eucalyptus and lavender. Soft music played in the background, the gentle sounds of rolling waves. We were greeted by the receptionist's warm smile as she checked us in.

First, we changed into plush white robes and lay side by side on plush, heated massage tables. We surrendered our tension to the skilled hands of the female Asian massage therapists. As good as it felt, my focus remained on Sienna—the way her shoulders eased when her eyes fluttered shut, the relaxing sighs escaping her lips.

Next, we headed to our private lunch, a table in a secluded spot near a crystal-clear waterfall. Sienna's smile spread from cheek to cheek as we feasted on fresh fruit and sipped champagne.

"How are you feeling? Your muscles loose? You feel relaxed?" I asked her before sinking my teeth into a fresh strawberry.

"I feel amazing. What about you?"

"Finally got those kinks worked on my neck, so I can't complain. But as long as you're good, I'm good."

"How have you been doing since... the hospital?" she probed.

"Maintaining."

"And the funeral?"

"In a few days."

"Do you want me there?"

"Of course I do."

"Good, because I was coming anyway, bighead," she said with a soft smile.

Being around Sienna was just what I needed to make my tension unravel. My lids fell shut as I breathed in the fresh, therapeutic air. For a second, it was almost as if I could feel Big Mama's presence surrounding me in a warm embrace.

I smiled. "She would've liked you, y'know."

"Your grandmother?"

"Yeah. She was always preaching to us about finding a good woman to settle down with."

"Too bad you're technically single," Sienna quipped.

"What?"

"C'mon, Ahsan. I know we're in public, but it's just us. You said when we were alone, we didn't have to pretend to be... y'know, who we're not."

I dipped my chin. "Yeah. You're right."

"But thank you for today. I really needed it. I wasn't going to tell you, but I started on a new piece a few days ago."

"Is it mine?"

"Maybe," she teased with a sly smirk. "You'll just have to wait and see."

Hours later, we watched the sky turn to bright, blended shades of pink and orange before dipping below the horizon.

"You wanna get in?" I quizzed as we approached the hot tub.

Sienna looked at the water with apprehension in her eyes. "Y-Yeah. Sure."

I noted her concern. "You don't have to."

"No. I want to. It's just... I haven't been in a hot tub since the night I went to that private party, and that nigga tried to kill me."

My hand found hers, grounding her. "I got you, Sienna. Every inch of your being is safe with me."

We slipped into a private hot tub, the warm water bubbling around us. Sienna leaned back, finding solace as she rested her head against my tattooed chest. My fingers traced her spine, wondering if she was dreaming or simply savoring the moment. I held her close as if time didn't matter. I kissed her forehead before slipping my hand down the front of her bikini bottoms underneath the water. She didn't stop me.

Instead, she turned her head to me and whispered, "What are you doing?"

"Giving you a better memory to erase the old one."

I spun her around and pressed her wet body against mine. We kissed passionately as I caressed her breasts. She massaged the back of my head while her nails dug into my back while I finger fucked her. A soft moan escaped her lips, and by the way she gripped my pickle, I knew she wanted me as much as I wanted her. The water sloshed as I pushed my fingers in and out of her, eager to suck her hard nipples poking against her bikini top.

Sienna purred, her soft moans echoing off the tiled walls surrounding us. "Oh shit, baby. Don't stop."

The bubbling water smacked against her ass as my hand slid her bikini bottoms to the side, replacing my finger with my hard dick with the intent of fucking her to sleep. For once, time didn't matter.

Sienna

The bright morning sunlight beamed through the floor-to-ceiling windows, warming Ahsan's silk bed sheets. I blinked a few times, momentarily forgetting where I was and how I'd gotten there before the memories of the night came flooding back. The thought sent a shiver down my spine. The inviting scent of his cologne lingered in the sheets, an intoxicating blend of blue cypress and sex.

As my mind raced, I outstretched every limb from my toned caramel fingers to my white-painted toes. After the day we'd shared at the spa and all the fucking we'd done at the spa and throughout the night when we'd gotten back to his place, it was safe to say whatever we were doing was more than just a business arrangement; it was a leap into uncharted territory that I wasn't sure either of us were ready for.

My gaze shifted to the private balcony, where the Vegas skyline seemed to stretch with no end in sight. As an artist, a part of me had always had my head in the clouds, but being in his private space felt like stepping into my wildest dream. *Is all this too good to be true?* Since Demario, I'd learned to be cautious around niggas and always protect my heart. Yet, lying here, swaddled in luxury, I couldn't help but wonder if God had finally blessed me with a real one.

As I eased out of his king-sized bed, my bare feet sank into the plush carpet underneath me. I caught a glimpse of a framed photograph on his dresser. It was him, younger, with a mischievous grin and his arms lovingly wrapped around his grandmother as she grinned from cheek to cheek. The sun's rays cast a warm glow across it, showcasing the minor dust particles in the air. I smiled briefly. It made me wonder more about who he was before his career took off.

The familiar aroma of brewing coffee wafted from the kitchen, enticing my senses and sending those questions to the back of my mind. I'd unravel the mysteries of his past some other day. I swiped up his T-shirt from the floor and slid it on to cover my naked body. I followed the aroma down the hallway, admiring the few pieces of modern black art decorating the walls. *So, he wasn't lying about possibly needing new art to add to his collection.* Ahsan's lavish apartment was much like him, in the sense it was quite a masterpiece. It had an open concept with minimalist décor, the perfect bachelor pad for a man of his stature.

I tiptoed across the marble kitchen floor, finding him standing at the stove, shirtless, with his back to me. The scorching morning sun spilled through the living room windows, casting almost a golden hue of light around his melanin-rich figure. I considered announcing myself but hesitated. Instead, I leaned against the marble countertop, watching him. I studied his movements, both practiced yet thoughtful, as he cracked an egg into a bowl, recklessly whisking it with more intensity than skill.

I watched, won over by his determination to chef it up when we both knew cooking wasn't his forte. There was a level of intimacy woven into the simplicity of his task. I wondered if he'd taken a page out of Larenz Tate's book in *Love Jones* and done the same for other women in the past, but something in the pit of my stomach said otherwise. That, and the burned waffles I noticed plated near the toaster. For a man of his stature, he could've easily ordered out, but instead, he'd chosen to wake up and stress himself out in a kitchen that looked like it was hardly ever used. Was I as remarkable as he made me feel? My insecurities knotted my stomach.

Ahsan glanced over his shoulder, his eyes finding mine. The tension between us instantly crackled like fireworks. He smiled lazily. "Morning," he said, voice still thick with sleep. "I, uh, tried to make you some waffles, but those shits are a bit... crispy," he admitted with a shrug.

I arched my brow. "That's dangerously close to romantic, Mr. No Strings Attached."

His eyes widened in surprise. "Only dangerously close? Guess a nigga gotta step up his game."

"I can't say I've ever seen anyone burn Eggos quite like that, but I guess you get an A for effort," I replied, stifling a giggle as I leaned against the counter.

He grinned, revealing a dimple as he slid the eggs into the pan. "Guess I'm better at other things."

His words sent ripples of arousal through me. *Ugh.* It was as if he were trying to get me pregnant with his words alone. I inched closer, drawn to him like a moth to a flame. "You'll hear *zero* complaints from me on that."

His gaze softened. "Good. So, scrambled eggs it is."

The interaction between Ahsan and me was a fragile tightrope walk of uncertainty and effortlessness. Questions hung in the air, fueled by the weight of our business arrangement and undeniable connection. Yet, there was also an ease I hadn't experienced with another soul. I'd heard of soul ties before, but what we shared was in another dimension. I stepped closer, looking into his eyes and wondering what else the morning would hold.

Before I could speak, his phone rang, interrupting our intimate moment. Ahsan stepped away, handing me the spatula to take over egg duty, as he answered the call. His voice was hushed from the living room. I cast a curious gaze in his direction, feeling a mixture of normalcy and disappointment.

He returned, his expression serious. "Go get dressed," he said, his gaze taking hold of mine. "After breakfast, you're riding with me."

His sudden change of plans stirred up a whirlwind of emotions and thoughts inside my mind, an entanglement of surprise, curiosity, and a dash of excitement.

"Um, okay."

"You good?" he asked.

I nodded. "Yeah."

"You sure?"

"It's just the first time I ever spent more than twenty-four hours with a client," I answered, breaking eye contact to plate the eggs.

"You feeling a way about that?" he inquired, walking up behind me and slipping his hands around my waist.

I looked over my shoulder, my gaze piercing his eyes as my heart fluttered like a million butterflies. "No. Forreal, I'm okay."

I found myself teetering on the edge of trust and cynicism. Ahsan's spontaneity was both charming and annoying. His words lingered in the forefront of my mind, a promise of an adventure beyond the privacy of his luxury apartment. But where? I knew he ran a trucking company, but the look on his face seemed more serious than a missed delivery. It made me question what kind of life he lived beyond his walls.

After we ate, I slipped into my clothes from the night before. I glanced back, catching a glimpse of his tousled bed sheets. As we stepped into the elevator, our hands briefly brushed against each other. It was sudden and accidental but sent a jolt of electricity from my fingertips to my toes. Our fingers intertwined for a heartbeat longer than necessary, and the air between us felt charged with promise. Just as the elevator doors dinged, Ahsan's lips found mine.

THE SHIPPING WAREHOUSE STRETCHED BEFORE ME, REVEALING itself as an unexpected answer to my questions regarding our destination. Ahsan pushed open the heavy metal door, unveiling rows of pallets of products lined up and waiting to be shipped across winding highways and state lines.

I glanced at him, curiosity etched in my brow. "Your trucking company?" I inquired.

He dipped his chin. "Welcome to my world," he said, gesturing at the rows of pallets.

I scanned the labels as we walked, noting the cardboard boxes carrying heavy-duty padlocks and products labeled as dangerous goods. "You have a little bit of everything in here."

"Yeah."

I followed him to the heart of the warehouse, where he stopped at a particular pallet. I squinted at one of the boxes with a black label on it. "What's this?"

"It's for a... niche market."

I tilted my head to the side. "A niche market? What does that mean?"

Ahsan squared his stance and stiffened his posture before looking me square in the eye. "I'm a kingpin, Sienna."

My limbs froze momentarily before I took a few steps back, eyes widening with surprise. I blinked rapidly, trying to process his words. A million thoughts raced through my head, but I was speechless. My eyes pinged from one pallet to another, unable to settle on anything in particular. I'd always known Ahsan had an edge to him, and I had suspected something darker lingering beneath the surface, but I had never suspected drug trafficking. My heart raced. The evidence was there, hidden in plain sight. He'd hidden his secret life behind the façade of his trucking business. The man I thought I was falling for now stood before me, revealing himself as something entirely outside of what I thought he was.

Anger and fear bubbled up, poisoning my veins. I could only think about Demario and how the streets had become his demise. *What if the Feds come for him and he goes to prison like Demario? What if they are already watching him and come for me too?* I wanted to turn away and call the whole fucking deal off right there on the spot. But I swallowed all those words down before they could escape my lips because anger wouldn't solve anything, and it damn sure wouldn't get me back into art school.

"Life's full of surprises," I finally uttered.

"Is all this too much for you to handle?"

"I don't understand why you're telling me this. You're not afraid I'll go to the cops or something?"

His grin was wicked. "You don't strike me as a stupid woman."

"I'm not."

"Good, then I should never have to worry about the Feds with you."

I shook my head. "You won't."

"Besides, I'm stepping down at thirty-five and handing this shit over to whoever wins the bet."

"What's next then? After thirty-five?"

"Full-blown legitimacy."

"Seriously? You could just give it up like that?"

Ahsan dipped his chin. "Absolutely. I've made my money. I've surpassed my goal. Anything beyond that is surplus. Besides, if you don't spend it, the government gon' tax it, and I'm ready to step into a new arena. Why is that so hard for everyone to believe?"

"Most niggas I know never get the chance to leave the game voluntarily. It's either a cell or a casket, at least the ones I know."

"I ain't most niggas. Plus, I had a plan, and I stuck to it. Most mothafuckas can't see past their first couple of steps. But me? I look at the whole board, analyze it from every angle, and then plan my moves accordingly, all falling into sync one after another."

"And I was a part of your plan?"

"You were never a part of my plan, Sienna. But that's only because I didn't know you existed before we met in the hotel that night."

"And if you had?"

He stepped closer, diminishing the gap between us as he brushed his fingers against mine. "Everything would revolve around you."

A trail of goosebumps rose on my arms. As honeyed as Ahsan's words were, they wouldn't wash away the scent of my haunted past still clinging to my skin. I completely shut down somewhere between Ahsan's confession and the past I thought I'd left behind. I'd danced the waltz of love and lies with Demario. He'd whispered promises and broken them, choosing the streets over me repeatedly. Yet, I believed him, hanging on to his every word that our love would be enough to get us through a fifteen-year bid, and that eventually I would become Mrs. Demario Barnes. But I wasn't the same young and foolish woman I was back then.

"I don't have a good track record with bad boys," I admitted.

"How so?"

"My ex... Demario. He got caught up trying to hit a lick, and he's locked up, doing a fifteen-year bid."

"How long he been in?"

"Five years."

"And you loved him?"

I shrugged. "Of course. He was my first love."

"And now?"

"Now?"

"Is that chapter of your life done?"

"Yeah, it is."

Ahsan traced the curve of my jaw, his thumb brushing away my invisible worries. "Listen, I understand your reservations. I know you see the world through a different lens. But like I said, I'm not most niggas, Sienna. I don't know how that nigga lived his life, but I would never let harm come to you."

I leaned into him with uncertainty etched in my features while fighting back tears. "But what if—"

"No buts, Sienna," he murmured. "I'd lie for you before I'd lie to you, especially when it comes to this shit. Trust me, I got you," he said, holding me close.

There was nothing left to say. I believed him.

Ahsan

The next day came, and I woke up craving Sienna as if she were my missing rib. She stayed at the forefront of my mind from my morning workout to my drive into the office. By the time I sat behind my desk, I was already scrolling through my phone, trying to find a local florist. Jules stood nearby, waiting to give me my morning update.

"Good news! The mayor's office sent over the finalized paperwork on the land. It's officially yours to start developing."

"That's wassup. I'm going to go by and check it out soon."

"And, um, the funeral director called about final arrangements for the funeral tomorrow, and he wanted to confirm you're still doing the eulogy."

I grunted. I'd begrudgingly agreed to give the eulogy at Big Mama's funeral and hadn't written down one word. I had less than twenty-four hours to come up with something encompassing who she was and what she meant to all of us.

"I'll give him a call back later," I responded.

"Okay."

"I need you to do something else for me."

"What's that?"

"Find a florist and have them send twelve dozen roses to Sienna's apartment."

She tapped my bouquet order onto her tablet with curiosity and envy across her face. "Twelve dozen? That's... over the top, don't you think? What's the occasion?" she quizzed with an arched brow.

I leaned back in my chair. "No occasion necessary."

Jules rolled her brown eyes, her jealousy barely suppressed. "Must be nice blowing money on jump-offs," she muttered.

My eyes narrowed, patience thinning with each passing second. "Jules, don't get your role in my life twisted. You may be my assistant, but my personal life is none of your fucking business," I barked.

Her chin dipped as her posture straightened, instantly realizing she'd gone too far. "I'm sorry, Ahsan," she said apologetically. "It won't happen again."

I stood to my feet, my six-foot-three frame towering over her. "Good. Now, remember your place or get replaced."

Without waiting for a response, I strode past her, leaving her to sit with her thoughts.

I GOT IN MY CAR AND TEXTED AMIR THE ADDRESS TO THE vacant lot, urging him to meet me there within the next half an hour. I punched the address into my GPS before leaving the office. Twenty minutes later, I sat in the driver's seat, parked near the lot, when my phone buzzed in the console. It was the funeral director. I sighed. *Fuck.*

I answered. "Hello?"

"Mr. Patton, hi. I'm just calling to confirm that you're all set to deliver the eulogy at your grandmother's funeral tomorrow."

My heart instantly tightened at the mention of Big Mama. I was still trying to put myself from underneath the ton of bricks her passing had stacked on me. The weight of responsibility hung on my shoulders as I cleared my throat. I knew she deserved a proper farewell.

"Yes. I'll be ready."

"Thank you, Mr. Patton. We look forward to receiving your family tomorrow for the service."

I hung up, staring out the windshield at the vacant plot ahead of me. Before I could collect my thoughts, Amir pulled up beside me. We both exited our vehicles and walked around to the front of them.

"Where the hell are we meeting in the middle of nowhere, nigga? You got a body in the trunk you need to bury?" he inquired.

I stood next to Amir with the plot of land stretched out before us. "No, nigga. It's official. This land is mine, Amir. The mayor's office sent over the finalized paperwork. We'll be breaking ground soon. This is the future home of my legacy."

Amir clapped me on the back with a warm smile on his face. "Congrats, bro. This is dope. You've got everything you wanted."

"I think you might be right about that."

"Big Mama would be proud."

I gave him a half smile. "Thanks."

"Speaking of Big Mama, everything set for the funeral tomorrow?"

"Yeah. Mr. Thompson from the funeral home has been blowing my phone up asking about the eulogy."

"You still feel up to it?"

"I thought I had more time, and now the funeral is tomorrow, but after all she did raising, feeding, and clothing us, I gotta honor her memory."

Amir nodded with understanding. "She'd want us to keep pushing forward. This land is a part of her legacy too. I know you gon' keep making her proud."

We clasped hands and drew each other in for our known dap/hug combo. "Bet."

Amir smirked. "And speaking of bet, how are things going with Sienna?"

"Everything's good."

"Yeah?"

"Yeah. I took her to the warehouse and told her the truth."

"The truth about what?"

"The game and my part in it."

Amir's playful smile faded, and the expression on his face turned more serious. "Why the fuck would you do that? Are you sure you can trust her?"

I nodded. "Yeah. I am."

He grunted. "Mmhm."

"What were you two talking about at the hospital the night Big Mama passed?"

"I straight up asked her if she knew about the bet. Hell, I even offered to pay her."

"And what did she say?" I quizzed, curious, yet already knowing the answer.

"She ain't say shit. I don't know if that's a good or bad thing."

I smirked, grateful that Sienna had held down our secret. "Nigga, it's a great thing."

***

Later that night, I sat on the balcony, taking a blunt to the face. I ashed it in my gold tray before I opened the notes section on my phone to write Big Mama's eulogy.

I looked up to the sky. "All right. Let's do this," I mumbled.

The words started flowing smoothly as I began to type.

Thank you all for being here today to celebrate the life of my grandmother, Violet Patton, or Big Mama, as we called her. Her life was rooted in three things: God, her unwavering faith, and her family. As many of you know, Big Mama raised me, my brother, and my cousin, Kendrick, practically from birth. And if anybody ever met Big Mama, she didn't hesitate to tell you how much she loved her boys. And we loved her right back. Over the years, she taught us a lot of things. I'd be standing up here all day running down that list. But if I had to pick one thing to focus on, she taught us that strength wasn't just about how muscular or how big you were. It was about your mind and the mental fortitude to stand tall when life is tearing you down.

I paused to scroll through my camera roll, halting at the photo of her on the screen. I'd never met someone who loved to smile as much as she did. I swiped back over to my notes and wrote some more.

Her kitchen was her sanctuary. And with a house full of three growing boys, she spent a lot of time in there. The scent of her pancakes on a Sunday morning or her sweet potato pie around the holidays could end any argument and make any scrape or busted lip heal quicker. She'd always say, 'The secret ingredient to life is love.' Although I know she's gone, I can still feel her presence. Her hugs are in the breeze, and her smile is in the warm sun rays. If she were here listening right now, I'd tell her that we love her and we're going to be okay. Her job is done, and now she can rest easy. The Patton boys will continue to keep her memory alive through us.

I swiped away a tear as I glanced at the crescent moon in the sky. I sat there, the weight of my words settling on my heart, which was both heavy and grateful. I drew in a deep breath before exiting the notes app. The next day, I'd have to stand up in front of my family and friends to honor the woman who shaped my future and showed me unconditional love that my biological mother couldn't even give me.

Sienna

The small Baptist church was heavy with grief. The wooden pews were lined in neat rows and filled with mourning family, friends, and acquaintances all gathered to pay their respects to Ahsan's grandmother, Violet Patton. Delicate white roses adorned her rose gold casket, their petals soft and pure. A small podium stood facing the congregation, draped with a white cloth and a gold cross down the front. I sat in the front pew surrounded by a sea of mourners draped in somber colors, hues of midnight blues, blacks, and grays. I clutched the program in my hand, reading about her life in the printed obituary.

Ahsan sat next to me, stoic, with his gaze fixed on the casket. His expression was a mix of sorrow and relief. His eyes were red-rimmed, and his hand trembled slightly while laced with mine. The pastor's voice echoed through the crowd, calling up Ahsan to do the eulogy. I knew how important of a moment it was for him. It was his final opportunity to pay his respects to the woman who'd raised him. He clutched his phone where he'd stored the eulogy he'd prepared for his grandmother and stood to walk toward the pulpit.

I held my breath, watching his every move as he glanced down at the casket adorned with white roses and drew in a deep breath. The eulogy began, and his deep voice instantly wavered as he spoke of his grandmother's unconditional love, wisdom, and the life lessons she'd taught them. Ahsan's love for his grandmother was evident, each word carrying weight. I listened intently, my heart swelling with emotion. Although I'd never met her, a part of me admired her through the stories alone. He stumbled over words as his eyes scanned the room, landing on his brother, who sat a couple of seats down from me, his eyes puffy from tears.

When he finished speaking, he stepped back, wiping a tear from his eye. The crowd erupted in applause. He stepped away from the pulpit, stepping toward the casket. He placed a white rose on top, then leaned down to kiss it before returning to his seat. The piano player started playing, and the choir rose, singing "Going Up Yonder." People in the congregation rose to their feet, voices joining the choir in a bittersweet sing-along.

I reached for his hand, intertwining our fingers before leaning in. "That was amazing. She would have been proud of you."

He nodded, his gaze still fixated on the casket. "I hope so," he murmured. "I wish she could have met you."

I squeezed his hand. "Me too."

As the funeral concluded, I stepped out of the church feeling a sense of closure. I'd gotten a glimpse of her loving spirit through Ahsan's kind words and gotten to experience a softer side of him. It was something I hadn't expected to see, but grief had a way of stripping people bare and wearing them down.

He'd proven himself to be more multifaceted than I imagined. Ahsan: the businessman by day, kingpin by night, with a soft spot in his heart that would always belong to his grandmother. His showing me his vulnerability instead of trying to swallow it down only made me feel closer to him. At that moment, it became clear that Ahsan and I had forged a connection deeper than anything money could buy.

We arrived at the small cemetery, where rows of headstones rose from the ground, each indicating a life that had since been recommitted to the earth. The pastor gave a closing prayer for peace over the immediate family in their time of sorrow before turning the services over to the funeral director to lower the rose gold casket into the freshly turned soil.

A few mourners lingered for a while, some tossing handfuls of soil or roses onto the wooden lid as a final farewell. Ahsan walked away, and I stood, giving him his space. I watched as he stepped toward the waiting earth, his hands trembling. He knelt, touching the fresh mound of dirt, and whispered something only he and his grandmother's spirit could hear.

"Yo, Sienna," Amir called out, walking over to my left.

"Hey. I'm so sorry for your loss. Your grandmother seemed like a real gem. I'm sorry I never got a chance to meet her."

"Thanks. She was," he answered, glancing around. "Where's my brother?"

I pointed in Ahsan's direction, watching him slowly make his way over to us. Amir outstretched his hand to dap up his older brother and hug him tightly.

"Yo, you did your big one up there today with that eulogy, nigga," Amir complimented him.

Ahsan nodded. "Thank you."

"You heard from XL? He need anything?"

"Nah. He good. He hung back at the church to prep the food for the repast."

Amir rubbed his stomach. "I can't wait to throw down. I'ma hit this blunt in the car on the way back to the church to make sure my appetite is ready."

"He told me he was making all her staple recipes," Ahsan responded with a knowing look.

"Big Mama always said food was love, right?"

"She sure did," he said, slipping his hand in mine. I stayed by Ahsan's side as we walked away from the gravesite back toward the car. "Have XL put two plates aside for us," he requested. "I'll pick them up from him later."

"You're skipping the repast?"

Ahsan dipped his chin. "Yeah. I need some space to process all this shit."

"Are you sure?" I asked him.

"Yeah. Let's go."

WE ARRIVED BACK AT AHSAN'S PLACE ABOUT TWENTY MINUTES later. He headed straight toward the balcony. I followed behind him, my heels clicking against the marble floor. The sun was low in the sky as we stepped onto the balcony. The bustling Vegas city buzzed below, but it felt like we were in another world up on his floor.

Ahsan leaned against the glass railing, his eyes fixated on the horizon miles and miles away. "Thank you for being here," he said, his voice thick with emotion. "I don't know if I could have faced today without you."

A sad smile crept up one side of my lips as I peeled off my heels and took my place beside him. "There was no place else I'd rather be," I responded, my gaze finding his.

He turned toward me, and I inched closer, mincing my steps. His arms encircled my waist, pulling me into his warm embrace. I rested my head of curls against his chest, feeling the steady thump of his beating heart. Instantly, the city and the grief all faded into the background. All I could feel was the warmth of his presence.

I reached up, brushing my fingertips against his beard. It was clear something deeper between us had taken root. My fingers trailed down his spine, finding the knots of tension that pained him. "Let me take care of you," I murmured soothingly. "Just for a little bit."

He shot me an understanding nod and took his seat. I stepped behind him and massaged his shoulders, rubbing away the day's heaviness. He sighed, leaning into my gentle touch. Ahsan rolled and lit a fresh blunt, the flame of the lighter dancing as we watched the day fade into the night. The smoke curled upward toward the sky into the fading sunlight. As the sun continued to dip lower, Ahsan turned to me and cupped the back of my neck. He drew in a long inhale. His eyes held a question, unspoken, yet I understood the assignment. I answered by pressing my lips to his and parting them to share the smoke in a shotgun before we kissed.

Ahsan

The groundbreaking ceremony for my new land had arrived. It was a bittersweet yet momentous occasion. With my thirty-fifth birthday a couple of months away, I still had one foot in the game and one foot out. The closer I got, the more ready I was to end the bet and let my family take charge so that I could fully focus on the new project and my relationship with Sienna. Although our relationship was fake, my growing feelings for her were anything but.

The air around me buzzed with anticipation. I stood tall in a custom-fitted black suit with a red tie. Sienna stood beside me, her hand tucked into the crook of my arm. Her brown orbs danced excitedly, and her makeup and curls only accentuated her Colgate smile. The mayor, clad in a navy pinstriped suit, stood at the podium, his voice amplified by the microphone near his lips.

"Ladies and gentlemen, we're gathered here today to celebrate the birth of a new partnership. Ahsan Patton, CEO of Patton Trucking Company, will work alongside the city of Las Vegas to turn this empty plot of land you see behind us into a thriving community over the next few years." He gestured toward the land behind us, where rumbling bulldozers waited patiently to break ground.

He continued. "From affordable housing to black-owned businesses, Ahsan, your vision for this new community is exciting and just what our city needs."

I shifted my weight from one foot to the other, feeling the weight of responsibility settle onto my shoulders like a cape. I glanced at Sienna, who squeezed my arm as the crowd applauded. My heart swelled with joy as I stepped toward the podium to shake the mayor's hand.

My firm and steady voice carried over the microphone. "Thank you, Mayor Dinkins."

The press took their position front and center, their cameras clicking and flashing to catch every photo opp. I'd never been comfortable in the spotlight in my line of work, but this was different. I glanced back at Sienna, her long, curly hair and soft brown skin catching the light.

The mayor and I lifted our shovels in ceremonial tradition. "To new beginnings," Mayor Dinkins cheered.

The shovels hit the ground with a thud, instantly breaking the soil. The flashing cameras captured the memorable moment. At that moment, the tension had been eased and replaced by joy. I knew there would be challenges ahead, but I also knew that the land was my first step in the right direction for my future.

As the ceremony concluded, the applause still rang in my ears. The mayor and the press had dispersed, and I turned to Sienna, ready to spend the rest of the evening celebrating with her in our birthday suits. But before we could get to that, her phone buzzed urgently in her hand.

She pressed the phone to her ear, eyes widening as she listened to the frantic person on the other line. "What? Calm down, Zyon. I can't understand you. You said what happened? What? Oh my God! Oh my God! I'm on the way!"

I stood at the ready. "What's wrong?"

Fear was etched into the lines of Sienna's face as her chest rose and fell with rapid breaths. "That was Zyon," she said, her voice tight with panic. "She said somebody broke into our apartment. I gotta go!"

My fists clenched. I'd imagined everything about this day, from the groundbreaking to the speeches and quotes for the press, but never this. "I'll drive you. Let's go," I announced, refusing her to walk into an unknown situation alone.

We sprinted to the car, my loafers kicking up dust. The drive to her apartment was a blur of anxiety and adrenaline. I prayed it was a false alarm. But as we reached the scene, the blue and red lights flashing against the brick building were the first indicator it was real. My gut twisted as I parked. *Fuck.* In the blink of an eye, we'd gone from the celebratory moments of my groundbreaking ceremony straight into the realm of real danger, and I didn't have my gun on me.

Sienna took off like a rocket into the building, sprinting up the stairs. I followed closely behind her, slowing my speed when I recognized the broken glass littered across the floor and the door hanging off its hinges. The police were scattered around, dusting for fingerprints and getting a record of everything stolen or damaged. Zyon stood in the kitchen, wrapped in a blanket, shaken but unharmed.

Sienna rushed to her side, arms enveloping her trembling cousin. "What the hell happened, Zy?" she probed, her voice raw with fear. "Are you hurt?"

Zyon's eyes darted to mine before shooting back to Sienna. "No. I'm fine," she answered, voice shaking. "I came home and found two fucking strangers standing in the middle of our living room. I screamed, and they shot off down the hall."

I surveyed the chaotic space, noting the overturned canvases, spilled art supplies, drawers yanked open, and overturned furniture. Sienna's eyes held worry. Without responding, she sprinted to the living room, where her clothes were strewn across the floor. She picked up an empty shoebox from underneath the couch and sank to the floor, tears blurring her vision.

"Oh my God!" she screamed. "It's gone. It's all gone!"

"What's gone? What did they take?" Zyon called out.

"The tuition money I'd been saving for art school! It's all gone! Every last fucking dollar! Who the fuck would do something like this to us, Zy? Who?"

Sienna's world had been shattered, and all I wanted to do was break the neck of the nigga that had disturbed her peace. Adrenaline surged through my veins, and my fingers sought hers, grounding her in her time of distress.

"Who all knows where you live?" I inquired, looking into her tear-filled eyes.

She wagged her head, unable to focus. "I don't know. No one, really. I don't know who could've done this."

We stood in the middle of the wreckage as the police worked. My thumb traced soothing circles on her palm, trying to soothe her frayed nerves. "We'll catch whoever did this," I promised, my anger simmering. "I won't let art school slip through your fingers, baby. Those mothafuckas might have taken your money, but they can't steal your purpose."

"Or your talent," Zyon added, walking over and squeezing her other hand.

"That's right."

Sienna clung to her cousin, tears streaming down her face. "Thanks," she whispered.

"Always, girl. You know I got your back."

Zyon stepped away and I pulled Sienna into my arms, fiercely determined to protect her at all costs. Our souls had forged a deeper bond that transcended monetary transactions and lust. From that moment forward, I'd carry the weight of her protection on my shoulders. I'd do anything to keep her safe.

Sienna

T wo and a half weeks later.

It had been a couple of weeks since the break-in at our apartment, and neither Zy nor I had been back in there since. Shit just didn't feel safe. Our home wasn't home anymore. While trying to find out who robbed us and work to break our lease early, Zy was staying with one of the girls from the club, and I'd been splitting my time between a hotel and Ahsan's place.

I glanced up, catching the silvery glow of the moonlight as I stood on the extended balcony of my hotel suite. The marble floor was cool against my feet as my easel stood before me. I dipped my brush into the palette of colors, delicately mixing them as I stared at the still photo on my phone of Ahsan sleeping. His grandmother's passing had left him in a somber mood, and I wanted to soothe his grief by presenting him with the custom painting he'd asked me for when we first met. I'd been painting it for him in secrecy for weeks and it was a few brushstrokes away from feeling complete.

I hadn't felt much like painting after the break-in and losing all my hard-earned money, but I knew I needed to start working on some new pieces just in case things took off for me after the exhibit at the Gallery at Forestbrook in a few days. Creating Ahsan's canvas was just the push I needed to get my creative juices flowing again. I mixed shades of espresso and mahogany, wanting to bring out his rich mahogany features. I admired how I captured the curve of his lips and the well-groomed beard covering his jawline chiseled to perfection. He was the finest nigga in the world, even in serene slumber. I dipped my brush into the warm, burnt sienna and brushed it across his full lips, wanting to capture their softness. I even captured the way his fingers curled and the way his delicate lashes rested against his closed eyelids.

Finally, I stepped back. My breath caught in my throat as my heart swelled with joy. The canvas was complete. I marveled at each delicate brushstroke, every detail carrying a piece of my heart and the feelings I'd never be able to put into words. It was more than art. It was my love letter to Ahsan, forged in shades instead of sentences. I signed my name in the bottom right corner of the canvas, branding my masterpiece before loosely covering it with a silk cloth.

As soon as I stepped back inside the suite, I went to wash my hands. My phone rang no sooner than I fell across the king-sized bed that dominated the room. I cracked my eyes open, catching the time and the name across the screen. It was well after one o'clock in the morning, and I was dead tired.

"Hello?" I answered.

"You up?" Ahsan asked.

"Do you know what time it is?"

"That's not what I asked you."

"I just laid down for the night. Wassup?"

"Don't fall asleep yet. I'm coming over."

"Right now? For what?"

"I need to give you something."

I smacked my teeth. "If your gift is dick, could you drop that package off sometime tomorrow *after* the sun comes up?"

"Chill, yo. It ain't that. Stay up for me, Sienna. I'll be there in half an hour," he instructed before ending the call.

I sighed heavily before sitting up and rubbing my eyes. My heavy footsteps trekked over to the thick, navy-blue curtains that framed the floor-to-ceiling windows and pulled them closed to hide the easel and canvas outside. Then, I raced to the bathroom to shower quickly and wash the paint residue off my skin. I hadn't expected him to drop by practically unannounced in the middle of the night.

Thirty minutes later, I heard a soft knock on the door. I swung the door open wearing a silk robe and my curls tousled.

"Hey," he said, his voice a low rumble. "I couldn't wait until morning."

"Why?" I quizzed, my voice a mix of curiosity and concern. "Is something wrong?"

Ahsan stepped inside, shutting the door behind him. He crossed the space, stopping in front of me with a rectangular box in hand with a red bow. "No. I needed an excuse to see you," he confessed. "But really, I just wanted to be near you."

I tilted my head to the left, studying him. "What's in the box?"

He handed it to me. "It's what I needed to give you. Open it."

I untied the red bow with trembling fingers. The lid lifted, revealing stacks of cash neatly arranged. My breath caught, and tears immediately welled up in my eyes. "Ahsan, what is all this?"

He sighed. "It's your full tuition money for art school. I want you to have it."

"But..." my voice cracked. "What about the bet?"

"No strings attached."

"I can't accept this. It's too much."

He shook his head. "You deserve it, Sienna. You've worked hard to achieve your dreams, and I respect your hustle—the late nights dancing at the club, the exhaustion of trying to save money for school. This is my way of saying you don't have to do that shit anymore."

I wiped away tears, my blurred gaze stationed on the money. As happy as I was that he'd offered to do something so sweet for me, I didn't feel right taking it. "This is more than anything I could have ever imagined someone giving me, but I'm sorry. I can't just take this."

"You're not taking it," he said firmly. "You're accepting it. There's a difference, and I'm not taking no for an answer."

A laugh slipped through my tears. "Okay, okay, fine. Thank you so much, Ahsan, seriously. You don't know what this means to me. Wait, but what's this?" I pointed to the bottom of the box, where a brass key lay among the bills.

"That is the key to my place. I have more than enough space for you to be comfortable. Leave this hotel and move in with me."

My eyes widened, and for a moment, everything seemed to slow to a crawl. "Wow, um. I don't know what to say. Can I think about it?" I asked.

"Of course," he said, brushing a curl from my face. "Take all the time you need."

I closed the box lid, knowing whether I said yes or no, Ahsan had already given me more than I could ever imagine.

"Since you're here, I have something for you too. Close your eyes," I instructed.

"For what?"

"Just do it, Ahsan. I got you," I promised, reaching for his hand and leading him around the bed. I pushed back the curtains and stepped outside onto the balcony. "Okay, watch your step. We're almost there."

"Fun fact about me: I like giving surprises. I don't like receiving them."

"Even good ones?"

"Any of 'em."

"Well, I think I can change your mind about that. Go ahead and open your eyes," I said.

Ahsan's eyes popped open as I pulled away the silk cloth. When he saw the canvas, his gaze softened. "Sienna," he whispered, his voice thick with emotion.

I laced my fingers with his. "For you. I just finished it, so it's still not fully dry yet, but what do you think?"

He stepped closer, his eyes tracing each line of the canvas, from the curve of his lips to the depth of his brown skin. "Wow."

"Well, have I officially changed your mind about surprises?"

He looked back at me and smirked before pulling me close. "Thank you for this. I love it. Nobody has ever given me anything so personal. I know exactly where I'm going to put it too," he stated with a sure nod.

"Where?"

"I'ma hang it right above the bed."

I smiled. "I think that's the perfect place for it."

"You got a name for it?"

"Yeah. I call it, *The Safest Place on Earth.*"

Ahsan smiled, and without hesitation, he leaned in and kissed me. It was a gentle press of lips against mine that sealed our bond.

I spent the next day getting my affairs in order—setting up a new bank account for the tuition money, getting my canvases ready for the upcoming art exhibit, reapplying for art school, and trying to decide whether or not I was going to take Ahsan up on his offer to move into his place. I figured Zyon could help me figure it out, so I saved my visit to her for last. She'd been crashing with one of the girls from the club, but because they worked different days, she mainly had the place to herself.

Before leaving the car, I flipped down the visor to check my reflection in the small mirror. My hair was styled in a neat twist-out, and silver hoop earrings dangled in my ears. I wore a fitted denim jacket, a white crop top, and matching denim jeans that hugged my curves.

I stood in the hallway outside of the apartment and hesitated. My fist trembled as I raised it to knock on the door. I'd been wrestling with the decision since he popped the question.

"Who is it?" Zy called out from the other side of the door.

"It's me, Sienna."

"Hold up a second."

The door finally creaked open a few seconds later, revealing Zy's familiar face. The scent of garlic and spices wafted past my nose. "Sienna. Wassup? What are you doing here?"

"I need to talk to you about something."

I stepped inside, glancing around the living room. I noticed the TV was on the sports channel. "You got company?"

"Nah. I was just in the kitchen cooking."

"And watching sports?"

She sucked her teeth. "I wasn't even paying attention to what was on. But wassup? Sit down, spill the tea."

"Ahsan asked me to move in with him last night."

Zyon's eyes widened. "You serious?"

"Yeah. And it's not like I haven't considered moving out and starting fresh anyway. I just wanted to know what you thought about it. I know we're trying to break our lease, and I just want to make sure you're still gonna be good regardless of whatever decision I make."

Before Zy could respond, I heard footsteps coming down the hallway. "I thought you said you didn't have company."

"Sienna, there's something I—"

I looked up to see Demario standing there, his eyes locking onto mine. Time froze. His caramel face bore the scars of a rough past, but his eyes still carried a hint of the reckless boy I once loved more than my next breath. His prison tattoos peeked out from under the sleeves of his faded black hoodie. His locs, once shoulder length, cascaded down the front of his hoodie, stopping midway down his chest. He was supposed to be locked away, paying for his mistakes for the next ten years.

"W-What the fuck? Why is he here, Zyon?"

"He's out," she said, her voice low. "But he's changed, Sienna. Maybe it's time you both faced the past."

"Baby girl, can please we talk in private?" Demario interjected, his voice gravelly.

I twisted my neck back toward Zyon and raised an eyebrow. "How long have you known?"

"For a few weeks now," she confessed.

"A few weeks? Are you fucking kidding me? And you didn't think to mention that shit to me?"

Her decision to remain silent weighed heavy. She knew Demario was out and knew he was there, but she still chose not to warn me. Zyon had a front-row seat to watch me rebuild my life after our breakup. She'd witnessed my tears and sleepless nights. She'd seen how I poured my pain into every piece of art I created. And yet, she'd chosen not to say a damn thing, seemingly choosing him over me.

"I know. I'm sorry! But since you're here, you may as well hear him out, okay? I'll give you two some space," she said before disappearing down the hall.

Demario inched closer, his moves a mix of caution and urgency. Just being in his presence overwhelmed me. Everything came flooding back, from the day we first met to the night he was arrested. I crossed my arms, trying to steady my balance.

"How are you?" he asked. "You look more beautiful than I remember."

"How the hell are you even out right now, Demario? It's only been five years."

"The DA on my case got arrested for some dirty shit, and all of his cases were reopened. So, here I am, baby girl."

"I'm not your baby girl, Demario. Not anymore."

"I've changed, Sienna. Forreal. I've forgiven you for leaving me when I needed you the most. I understand why you couldn't hold me down."

I scoffed. "You forgive me? You think that shit was easy for me? Watching you walk away in handcuffs, nigga? Seeing you get sentenced to a fifteen-year bid?"

Demario's chestnut brown eyes softened. "I'm sorry. I didn't mean to upset you. I'm just trying to show you I'm not the same nigga I was five years ago, Sienna. Prison changed a nigga. The only thing it didn't change was my love for you, baby girl."

I clenched my fists. "Stop calling me that, nigga! How dare you just drop back into my life like this all unannounced!"

"I wrote you a letter telling you I was getting out. I thought you knew."

"I didn't know shit because I didn't read shit, Demario. It's been years. I've moved on. I can't go back."

"For the last five years, all I've dreamed of is us picking up where we left off and starting over from the beginning. I wanna do shit the right way this time, Ba—Sienna," he corrected himself.

My anger flared through my nostrils. "You don't get to show up out of the blue and rewrite our history. I've rebuilt my life brick by brick without you, and I plan to keep it that way."

Demario stepped closer, desperation in his sorrowful brown eyes. "Sienna, please. All I'm asking for is one more chance."

"No!" I said, my voice rising. "And fuck you for looping my fucking cousin into your shit! Stop trying to use her to get to me! There are no second chances, all right? I'm done."

Our heated words ricocheted off the walls as my heart thudded. I stormed out of the apartment, leaving Demario and my deceiving ass cousin behind.

Ahsan

Sienna called to tell me she was on her way to my place. I could hear it in her voice. Something was off. My cleaning lady had left my apartment spotless and filled with the fresh aroma of vanilla candles as I waited for Sienna's arrival. When she stepped inside twenty minutes later, I smiled at her. Her eyes narrowed. One look and I could all but see the emotions simmering beneath her melanated skin.

"Hey," I said, wrapping my arms around her. "You good?"

She shrugged, avoiding my gaze. "Yeah, just tired, I guess. It's been a long day."

I led her to the couch, and she wasted no time folding her petite frame into its soft cushions. She let out a long exhale. "Listen, Amir's turning thirty this Saturday. And it wouldn't be him without a lavish ass party to celebrate. You'll come, right?"

Sienna's exhaustion flared into instant irritation. "Your brother's birthday? Seriously? You do know that clashes with my art gallery show, right?"

I blinked, taken aback. "Oh shit. I didn't realize—"

"Of course, you didn't," she snapped, rolling her eyes. "You're always thinking about your family and your commitments. What about mine? No one looks out for me like they say they do. I'm surrounded by a bunch of self-serving mothafuckas."

My brow furrowed. "What the hell is wrong witchu, Sienna? Why are you—"

"Being a bitch?" she finished my sentence. "Because life isn't all about you, Ahsan, and I'm tired of pretending it is. I work my ass off, too, and for what? To be robbed? To be overshadowed by your brother's birthday? He gets one every year just like the rest of us!" She hissed.

My chest deflated with a hard sigh as I reached for her hand. "Yo, baby, I'm sorry. I didn't mean—"

"You never do," she interrupted. "You're selfish, just like everyone else. And there's no need to call me baby. We ain't in public. We can stop pretending."

My eyes searched hers for the truth, but all I got in return was a distant gaze. It was easy to see her mind was elsewhere. "Tell me what's really going on."

She hesitated then sighed. "I just... feel like I'm drowning right now," she said finally. "I just need to take a shower and go to bed."

"Okay," I whispered before kissing her forehead. "I'm gonna go to the warehouse, so I might not be here when you wake up."

"I'm a big girl, Ahsan. I can take care of myself," she snapped. "Good night."

I watched her disappear down the hall, torn between wanting to press her to tell me what the hell was going on and giving her the space we both knew she needed. I stood back briefly before grabbing my keys and heading toward the door. As I closed the door behind me, I wondered if I'd made the right choice in asking her to move in with me. But Sienna's face—the way she'd smiled when I gave her that box of tuition money—reminded me why I'd leaped in the first place. Being in love wasn't about convenience; it was about choosing to hold the other person down, even when shit wasn't sweet. *Holy shit. I fuckin' love her.*

The early morning sunlight filtered through the curtains as I watched Sienna sleep, noting each gentle rise and fall of her chest and how her lips curved slightly when she was most peaceful. Her mood had been distant, and I couldn't help but wonder if there was something else I could do to bridge the gap between us and figure out what was gnawing at her. I placed a gentle kiss against her forehead before climbing out of bed and getting ready to go into the office.

I trekked into the office, my heart and mood heavy, and Jules instantly picked up on the dip in my mood. "What's eating at you?" she inquired, leaning against the doorframe.

I hesitated then sighed. "It's Sienna. Her mood's been off. She came at my neck and called me selfish last night."

Jules raised an eyebrow. "Selfish? Why? What happened?"

I recounted the argument, the clash between Amir's thirtieth birthday party and her art gallery show. Jules listened intently. "Maybe she's stressed," she suggested. "Women are known to be complicated creatures, you know."

I chuckled. "Yeah. Tell me about it."

"Sometimes, we say things we don't mean in the heat of the moment. And other times, we say exactly how we feel. I don't know the girl. Maybe she's struggling with something deeper that has nothing to do with you."

I dipped my chin. "I just want to understand her."

Jules stepped closer, closing the door behind her. "You know, I've been working for you for years. I've *never* seen you seriously date anyone, but this... you... it's different. Ahsan. You're different. You're invested in this girl."

I frowned. "That's an issue?"

She hesitated then blurted it out. "Maybe not for you, but it is for me when I have feelings for you. I've kept them to myself out of respect for you and the workplace. But hearing about you with

Sienna... I'm gonna be real with you. It hurts," she confessed, her eyes misting with tears.

I blinked, stunned. "Jules, I—"

"Don't," she interrupted, holding out her hand to stop me. "It's obvious you're going to choose her. But it's hard, okay? Knowing that I've been invisible to you all this time, and then this random woman can fall out of the sky, and you hand your heart right over to her. I mean, what even makes you think she deserves it? Deserves you?" Jules stepped closer, closing the gap between us. She placed her hands on both sides of my face and looked into my eyes. "I love you, Ahsan. I've been in love with you for years," Jules confessed before quickly lunging for my lips.

I pulled away, smearing the feel of her sticky lip gloss off my lips as I drew in a deep breath. "Jules, you're an incredible assistant. You've been loyal from the beginning, and you know that means everything to me. But Sienna is my girl, and ain't shit about that changing," I confirmed. "If you can't respect that, you can find another job."

Her shoulders sagged as she looked away to wipe her eyes. "I'm so sorry. I shouldn't have done that. I know. It's just... I always thought you'd think of me whenever you were ready to settle down. The realization that it will never happen stings like a bitch."

I realized how embarrassed she must have been, and out of respect for our working relationship, I held back from cussing her ass out like I wanted to. "Like I said, I appreciate you, Jules. But I won't jeopardize what I'm building with Sienna for nobody. Take the rest of the day off to get yourself together. When you return in the morning, work on finding your replacement."

The weekend rolled around. The night air was warm as I stood outside the venue of Amir's thirtieth birthday party, clutching a single red rose for Sienna. She'd gone to her art exhibit and promised to meet me at the party afterward. I looked up to see Sienna walking over, her eyes widening in surprise when she noticed the velvety crimson petals. Her skin glowed underneath the lights, and her curls perfectly framed her face. I extended the rose toward her, a nervous smile tugging at my lips.

"Hey, beautiful." I greeted her, my voice low and intimate. "Congratulations on your art exhibit. How did it go?"

Sienna's eyes softened as she accepted the rose. "Thank you," she said. "It was incredible! I sold all my paintings!" She cheesed.

My heart swelled with joy. "I knew you would. You're amazing," I murmured, pulling her close. Our lips met in a sweet, lingering kiss. "How have you been?" I asked, brushing my thumb over her soft cheek. "You've seemed off lately."

Sienna hesitated then sighed. "I know, and I'm sorry. I promise we'll talk about it after the party."

"Okay. Bet. As long as you good, I'm good."

She leaned into me, her head resting on my shoulder. "Thank you for being patient with me and believing in my artwork."

I kissed her forehead. "Always," I vowed. "Now let's go inside."

The hotel ballroom shimmered with crystal chandeliers overhead as people laughed and danced while getting their drink on. Sienna's eyes were bright as she leaned into me. She seemed to be in better spirits, which I appreciated. I felt a surge of relief. Maybe things were finally turning around.

My brother, the birthday boy, stepped onto the stage with the mic in his hand. The DJ cut the music, and the crowd hushed, anticipating his speech. "Thank you all for being here," he said, his baritone voice echoing throughout the large room. "Let's give it up for me and thirty mothafuckin years, baby! It's a milestone!"

The crowd cheered, and Sienna squeezed my hand. I smiled down at her. It felt good to be on good terms again. "I'm glad I made it," she whispered.

Amir cleared his throat before he continued, "But tonight, I have an announcement." He glanced at the woman beside him, his spitfire ex, Brandi. Her eyes widened with surprise. "Baby, we've had our ups and downs, but I've realized life's too short to waste time. When you know, you know. So, here goes." He pulled a velvet box out of his back pocket before dropping to one knee in front of everyone. "Will you marry me?"

The crowd gasped as he cracked open the box. The ring sparkled underneath the crystal chandeliers. She nodded, tears streaming down her face. "Yes, baby," she said, her voice trembling. "Yes! I'll marry you!"

The room erupted in applause, Sienna included. Mixed emotions swirled around as I watched Amir slip the ring onto his fiancée's finger. There was pride for his happiness mixed with a pang of doubt behind his decision to marry someone he could barely stay on good terms with for more than a few months at a time. Yet, I clapped, smiled, and prepared to wish them well, knowing damn well they'd need it.

The DJ got the music spinning back to life, playing the remix to "Let's Get Married" by Jagged Edge and Run DMC. Everyone hit the center of the room to celebrate the happy couple on the dance floor. The room pulsed with music and laughter. Sienna's hand found mine again, tightened her fingers around mine, and I knew she felt it too. The shit between us was far from fraud. My eyes landed on the groom-to-be standing near the bar, his eyes delighted. At the same time, I noticed Jules stumbling into the party. Something about her looked off as she swayed over to him and gripped his arm.

"Come on, let's go congratulate my brother," I told Sienna.

We made our way through the crowd over to the bar. I shot my eyes over to Jules. Her cheeks were flushed, and she looked like she'd been drowning her sorrows in a bottle of vodka.

"Congratulations, bro," I said, dapping Amir up and interrupting their conversation.

Amir hugged me, and we swayed from left to right. "Thank you, man. Thank you."

"What made you wanna pop the question?" I inquired.

"Shit, nigga. After Big Mama died, I just realized life was too short. So, I brought her some sage and a lighter and told her we were both toxic and we needed to burn one and then burn some fuckin' sage to clear the air and start fresh."

"Yeah, congrats, Amir! That's amazing news!" Sienna added before reaching out to hug him.

"Thank you. From the way you got my brother cheesing, I'd say y'all might be right behind us," he replied.

"Hold up," Jules interrupted. "What did I miss?"

"I proposed to my girl a few minutes ago."

Jules's glossy eyes popped wide. "What? You're engaged, Amir?" He grinned. "Yup!"

"Holy shit! Wow! I guess congratulations are in order for both Patton brothers. Everybody gets a happy ending, even if one was paid for, right?" Jules blurted out.

Our circle of four fell silent as everyone traded muted glances. Amir's brow creased. "What? What is she talking about?"

I sucked my teeth. "Ignore her, nigga. She's drunk."

"You do know," Jules interjected, her voice way too damn loud, "the bet you two made was rigged, right?"

Amir frowned. "What? How the fuck did you know about the bet?"

"Because I handled Sienna's initial payment. You know, the one he paid her to go along with him on this bet. Scholarship fund, my ass." She snickered.

My brother's expression went blank. "What are you saying?"

I jumped in. "Yo, mind your fucking business, Jules."

She belted out a grated laugh. "Your brother's perfect little love story? It's all bullshit. Sienna's in on it. Something didn't feel right to me about how quickly they got together, so I logged into Ahsan's iCloud account, read their text thread, and found out everything."

Amir's furrowed gaze darted to Sienna, who stood eyes wide. "Is that true?"

Sienna stepped forward, her voice steady. "She's obviously drunk and delusional," she said. "Let's not—"

He cut her off. "Is it fucking true?"

"Yo, Jules, you're way out of fucking line right now. Is this about what happened at the office earlier this week?"

"What happened at the office?" Sienna asked, turning her attention to me.

Light on her feet, Jules swayed to the beat, her grin wicked. "Fuck it. Since we're t-telling the truth, let's t-tell it all," she slurred.

"Fine. I'll tell them that you came on to a nigga, and I put you in your fucking place. But obviously, that wasn't enough for you so you had to bring your dumb ass in here and embarrass yourself."

"Drunk or not, is she telling the truth, nigga?" Amir asked, jumping back into the conversation to get the answer to his question.

"It is the truth, but it's not what you think."

"Bullshit! We made a fucking deal, nigga. And you cheated to make sure you'd win? Why? Because you don't think I can do this shit! This ain't about my inability to run shit. It's about you not wanting to take your hands off the fucking wheel!"

"Yo, chill. Not here, nigga. We'll talk about this some other time," I said, catching the eyes pinned on us.

Amir's anger flared. "Fuck that, nigga! You a fraud ass nigga! You and your bitch, get the fuck out of my party!"

"Watch your fuckin' mouth, mothafucka. Birthday or not, I will still fuck you up," I warned.

Sienna reached for my hand, and I snatched it away. "C'mon, Ahsan. Let's just go."

"Fuck that!" I yelled.

"I said get the fuck out!" Amir roared.

His fist connected with my jaw, and I stumbled back, colliding with a nearby table.

"Enough!" Amir's fiancée called out as she ran over to the commotion. "This is my baby's birthday and our engagement party! If he said get out, you need to get out!"

I held my jaw, ready to turn into the Hulk on his ass. "Fuck this shit! You want me gone? I'm gone!"

I stomped away from the glittering party with Sienna hot on my trail. I stepped into the night, disappointment clinging to me like a second skin. Amir's reaction hit me like a tidal wave. No matter my intentions, my guilt felt like an anchor dragging me down. I'd expected shock, maybe even disappointment, but not the raw fury I was met with. I was still pissed off at how things went down so publicly. Family business was supposed to happen behind closed doors. That was how we were raised. But he'd put his hands on me, and that nigga was gon' have to see me about that, blood or not.

The party's music still rattled in the distance. After a few paces, Sienna reached out and touched my arm. "Ahsan, slow down. Are you okay? Let me see your face."

I wasn't, but I lied anyway. She had been caught in the crossfire, having her loyalty tested. I appreciated her willingness to ride for me, though. "I'm fine," I grumbled. "I need some air."

I trekked along the moonlit path, the night air cool against my skin. Amir's face flashed before me, the hurt and rage in his eyes, the trembling fists. The sucker punch, his words spat with malice.

Jules's confession also lingered in the back of my mind, a bitter aftertaste after everything that had gone down. Reading my private messages behind my back? I hadn't seen her betrayal coming from a mile away. Even before I hurt her feelings, she'd loved me in silence, and I'd never noticed. How many chances had I missed to see her as more than my assistant? I grappled with her confession and my rejection's impact on my relationship with her, Sienna, and my brother. It was all fucking tangled and knotted up. I felt a mix of betrayal and disappointment. She'd driven a massive wedge between Amir and me. As far as I was concerned, we had no path forward. As for Amir, I couldn't undo the past. But I could give the nigga his space, let him bask in the happiness of his engagement, and regain his trust when the time was right.

Sienna

I let Ahsan blow off some steam, hanging back a few paces behind him, ready and waiting for whenever he was prepared to talk. I knew he was sick over how things went down between him and his brother, not to mention his assistant blowing us up like that out of nowhere. I couldn't ignore the damage she'd caused.

Ahsan finally turned around. His eyes locked with mine as he shook his head. "You ready to go?"

"Yeah. I can drive if you want."

"I'm good now."

"You sure? That was... a lot back there."

"My only concern is him." He glanced at me then walked back the way we came.

"And you're my concern, Ahsan," I called to his back.

He stopped dead in his tracks and turned to face me. "I'm sorry."

"Don't be. I just want you to know that I'm here. I wanna be a safe space for you like you've been for me."

I watched his gaze fall from my eyes to the concrete beneath us. His expression was tense, and his eyes were red. "You know how stubborn that nigga can be. It's all over a stupid bet we had no business making in the first place. I understand why he's mad, though. I rigged it. I cheated."

"Did you have a good reason to do what you did?"

"Yeah. I didn't want him to throw away his life to the game. You saw him put a ring on that girl's finger. He's got something to lose now, Sienna. And the game will take everything he loves. I wanted more for him than that."

"Have you told him any of this?"

"No."

"Then maybe you should."

"His hotheaded ass don't wanna hear from me right now."

"Maybe not, but you'll already know exactly what to say when he's ready to."

"Thanks, and thank you for holding me down in there. I didn't want you caught up in it. I feel like shit for dragging you into this mess," he confessed.

"Hey, we're a team, remember? And I've got your back, period. In time, I know you two will make it right."

"And what about Jules? Now I'm down an assistant."

"Don't worry about her right now. She's not worth your peace."

Ahsan leans in, his forehead touching mine. "You've held me down through everything: the gala, the loss of Big Mama, the groundbreaking. It can't all be because of the bet, can it?"

I looked into Ahsan's eyes. Things between us may have started under false pretenses, but it was no secret that feelings had gotten involved since we'd started the bet. As badly as I wanted to confirm his feelings and tell him it wasn't, hearing Ahsan put his feelings into words only made me feel bad about my role in it all. I couldn't help but feel like I should've stuck to my guns from the beginning and walked away when I still could. But I was blinded by the money in the beginning.

But now that I knew I had deeper feelings for him, a part of me considered taking a step back from his life so that he and his brother could make amends. They were fine before I came into the picture.

The old saying, *if you love something, let it go*, kept repeating in my head, but I couldn't kick him while he was already down by telling him I didn't think us moving in together was a good idea. The thought of staying away from Ahsan for more than a few days at a time made my stomach churn. We were supposed to be each other's escape, but I realized I'd been drowning in an entire ocean of him since we'd met. Never did I think I'd want him the way I did, but there was no mistaking it: I was head over heels in love with Ahsan Patton.

I cleared my throat, pulling myself out of my thoughts. Instead of answering his question, I decided to take the time to tell him what had been going on with my mood, as promised.

"Do you still wanna know what's been going on with me?"

A look of concern was etched across his face before he replied, "Yeah. Wassup? You know you can tell me anything."

I took a deep breath while fidgeting with my fingers. "Well, first, I need to apologize to you. I went to talk to Zyon about moving out and was ambushed by my ex. It was unexpected as hell. Last I knew, he was still locked up. Seeing him again knocked me clean off my square. But that didn't give me the right to take my frustrations out on you, and I'm sorry about that."

"Is this nigga going to be a problem?"

I swung my head. "No. I made it clear that whatever we had was in the past. My only focus is my art."

"And your cousin?"

I sighed. "We don't always see eye to eye, but I hope she comes to her senses about being around him. She's always had a soft spot for him. She used to date his cousin back in the day before he was killed. After he passed, I don't know... It was like something in her died too. She's been pressing me to reconcile with my ex since we broke up five years ago. Some sort of misplaced loyalty."

Ahsan grunted. "You sure that's all it is?"

"Yeah."

"Why did you two break up?"

"I was young and couldn't handle the pressure of being with someone who was locked up for fifteen years. Plus, he didn't like that I was stripping at the club to make ends meet. His jealousy got to be too much for me to bear. It reached the point where we would argue every time he called. Who the fuck wanna put money on someone's books just to argue?"

Ahsan dipped his chin. "How did he get out after only five years?"

"He said something about the DA who prosecuted his case got brought up on charges, so now all of the cases he presided over are being reopened."

"We need to set some ground rules, Sienna. I don't trust that nigga or your cousin, and I don't want you near them. Promise me you'll stay away."

"Listen, I know you're worried, but I can handle myself. I've been through a lot, and I won't let my past shake me. I've come too far."

He sucked his teeth. "It's not about whether or not I believe you can handle yourself, Sienna. It's about never having to. I don't want you in any situation where you have to deal with that kind of stress or potential danger, all right?"

"Ahsan, I hear you, but even though Zyon pissed me off by not telling me about Demario getting out or being around her, I still need to resolve things with her. She's the only family I have out here, and we live together. I can't just cut her off. As for my ex, I told you I made it clear to him that shit between us is over, dead, buried, and never coming back to life," I confirmed.

"Blood or not, if she's pushing you toward a nigga who's bad for you, she ain't got your best interests at heart. And your ex, I don't like an unpredictable nigga. I'm not about to let anything happen to you, Sienna. Not on my watch."

I reached out to hug him. "Thank you. I promise I'll be careful, okay?"

I wasn't used to having someone around who wanted to shield me from the shadows of my past. His stern approach was somewhat comforting but also a little suffocating. As much as I appreciated Ahsan's protective nature, I needed to ensure he understood I wasn't a damsel in distress. Just because he'd met me at a financial low didn't mean I wasn't strong or incapable of making a way for myself without his muscle or his money.

Yet, an undeniable sense of relief enveloped me like a warm blanket on a cold winter night. Relief that, for the first time, I didn't have to face my demons alone and that I had a real nigga watching my six. It was a new feeling that would take me some time to find my footing in, but I welcomed the renewed sense of protection.

Ahsan

It had been a few days since everything had gone down at Amir's party. He hadn't returned my phone calls or texts, so I decided to pull up on him. I stepped out of the elevator. The plush hallway carpet muffled my footsteps before I halted outside his hotel room. I drew in a deep breath before my knuckles collided with the door.

"What?" Amir called out from the inside.

"Yo, it's me. Can we talk?"

The door opened, revealing Amir with resentment etched on his face. He wore a faded hoodie and had a duffel bag over his left shoulder. "Fuck do you want?" he griped.

"You going somewhere?"

"I'm moving back in with Brandi. Grown men gotta do grown-up shit, right?"

I cleared my throat while swallowing my pride. "Look, I know shit ain't been sweet between us lately, but we're blood. We can't let one disagreement tear us apart."

"Blood? You mean the same blood that didn't believe in me? That thought I'd fail whenever you stopped being too scared to step away from the game?" he barked.

"Nigga, I'm telling you it wasn't like that. I was just trying to protect you."

Amir scoffed. "You think I didn't see through your lies from the beginning? I grilled her ass at the hospital because I knew something was up! You didn't believe in me from the jump, nigga. You never fucking did!" he argued.

"That's not true. I've always believed in you. You're my little brother."

"Believed in me? You got a funny way of showing that shit. Well, guess what, nigga? I'm a changed man. I'm engaged now and moving back in with my girl. I don't give a fuck what you think about me."

"Can you blame me for having my doubts? You pick and choose when you wanna be a clown and when you wanna be a grown-ass man. You always have."

"I told you I'm a changed man."

I huffed, ready to stop arguing. "Listen, I was wrong, all right? I shouldn't have rigged the bet in my favor. I was scared that you'd have to give up what you love to stay on top. You know you don't get but one choice in this life, Amir. It's the game or nothing."

"You think I don't know that?"

I sighed. "Can we please put this shit behind us? We're family."

Amir scoffed. "Family? Mr. Mothafuckin Businessman is so good at saying all the right things, but your actions? You're all cap, nigga."

I felt my patience running thin. "Goddamnit, I've apologized to your black ass a hundred fucking times. I'm here now, trying to fix this shit. But if you won't fucking listen—"

"Then fuck it then! Get the fuck outta here, nigga. I ain't ask you to come here in the first place! I'm good without you," Amir barked.

I clenched my jaw before turning away. I stormed down the corridor, my shoulders weighing heavy with regret. I knew we'd fix our issues someday, but not anytime soon.

Sienna

Zy and I hadn't spoken since the night I stormed out after being ambushed by Demario. I got word that our landlord agreed to let us break our lease due to the break-in, and I was headed over to pack up the rest of my things and move them into the hotel until I got around to finding a place of my own and giving Ahsan back his key.

I walked into the apartment and stood frozen in the doorway, my heart pounding. One look around, and I could smell the betrayal in the air.

"Zyon?" I quizzed.

She turned from the kitchen, eyes widening as she saw me. "Sienna? What are you doing here?"

My eyes darted over to Demario sitting in the living room. "And what the fuck is he doing here?"

"It's not what you think."

I scoffed while folding my arms across my chest. "It never is."

When I looked at him, I snarled. His presence was like a festering wound that refused to heal.

He smirked while lounging on the couch. "Surprise, surprise, baby. Did you miss me?" he teased.

I clenched my fists as a million different scenarios ran through my mind. He always did have a way of slithering through life and leaving chaos in his wake. *Did this mothafucka have something to do with breaking into my apartment? Was Zyon in on it too?*

"Look, just stay the fuck out of my way, all right? I just came here to pack my shit," I stated.

"Don't worry, I didn't touch your precious art supplies."

"Whatever."

I stormed toward the corner of the living room where my things were and started packing my canvases, brushes, clothes, and everything else. When I made my way down the hall to the bathroom, Zyon followed, pleading at my back.

"Sienna, please listen. Demario is trying to change," she said in his defense.

I snapped my neck at her, ready to cave her face in and hopefully knock some sense into her ass. "Change? Bitch, are you that blinded by false loyalty or just that fucking dumb?"

"Excuse me?"

"Of all people, I really thought I could fuckin' trust you. But fuck it! Do whatever you want. I don't care! Just don't get too comfortable around that nigga, and don't call my ass when shit hits the fucking fan! Because when it does, that's on you!" I warned.

It was then that I realized family could bring you down quicker than a stranger would. There were snakes in my garden, and I refused to be bitten again. I shoved as much shit into my bags as I could before pushing past Zyon and dragging them out of the apartment, leaving her and Demario behind. Zyon's actions were living proof that I had to watch my family harder than I had to watch my enemies. After that encounter, my guard was up higher than the Great Wall of China. I decided to change my number and be more careful about who I allowed into my personal space in that season of my life.

After an hour of driving around the city with tears streaming down my face and my heartache threatening to swallow me whole, I found myself standing at Ahsan's door, clutching some of my belongings. The door opened, and Ahsan stepped aside to let me in. The minute he looked at me, he didn't say a word. He pulled me into a tight hug. It was like our souls were connected on this planet and the next.

"Shh, it's okay, baby. You're safe now," he whispered before kissing the top of my head.

I buried my face in his hard chest, sinking into the warmth of his touch. With Ahsan, I was exactly where I wanted to be.

Ahsan

Two weeks faded by since Sienna had officially moved in with me. We were doing well, adjusting to each other's ebbs and flows. But as for my brother and me? Well, I was still uneasy about where our relationship stood. We hadn't said more than two words since I pulled up on him at his hotel. Whenever we ended up in one another's presence, we used XL as our buffer and spoke through him.

Sienna fit into my life seamlessly. She was the only sliver of peace I had. I stepped out onto the balcony, my eyes drawn to her easel. She stood there focused, concentration lost somewhere in her unfinished painting.

"You're up early," I said, walking up behind her and slipping my hands around her waist.

She smiled with her brush in hand. "When inspiration calls, I gotta answer."

I leaned against the railing. "What's this one about?"

Sienna gestured toward her half-finished masterpiece. "I don't quite know yet. It's speaking to me. I'm just not sure I know what it's trying to say yet."

"Well, I didn't come out here to disrupt your vibe. I've got some business to handle down at the warehouse. You know what it is."

"How long will you be gone?"

"I'll be back later this evening," I confirmed.

"Hmm. I should hopefully be done with this by then. I'm torn. Should I attempt to cook dinner or order takeout?"

"Tough choice. When you decide, call me and let me know. I can pick it up on my way in if it's takeout. Deal?"

"Is this your slick way of trying to get out of washing the dishes tonight?" she quizzed, raising an eyebrow.

I smirked before kissing her forehead. "I'll be waiting."

Her eyes lingered on me for a moment. "Be safe, Ahsan."

"Always."

I headed toward the door, leaving Sienna with her unfinished canvas and creative mind. Outside at my car, I slid into the driver's seat as the engine purred to life. My phone vibrated in my palm, and I glanced at the screen. It was my cousin, XL.

"Yo," I answered on the third ring.

"Wassup, fam? You good?"

"I'm straight."

He sighed before his voice crackled through my car speakers. "I can't believe it's been a month since Big Mama left us."

I gripped the steering wheel. Hearing him say it was the first time I'd thought about it. "Damn."

"You talked to Amir?"

"Nah."

"You niggas still haven't patched shit up yet?"

"Nah. Still radio silence over here. I still can't believe that mothafucka sucker punched me at his party."

"Yeah, well, life is too short for petty grudges, nigga. You know that. And you know if Big Mama were still here, she would've said the same thing. You gotta make things right, Ahsan. Family is all we got."

I glanced in my rearview mirror, remembering Big Mama's

wisdom and Sock it to Me cake she'd always make us to help solve every fight. My chest deflated with a hard sigh. "You're right. I'ma fix it."

"Good. That's all I wanted to hear. You good with your pickup route?"

"Yeah. I'm about to start making my rounds now," I told him.

"All right, bet. I'm at the warehouse with Bradley and Rico loading up the trucks to make the drops now. Be easy."

"You too," I replied before ending the call.

XL's words made me detour on my way to the first stash house and stop by Big Mama's gravesite to visit her. After sitting in peaceful silence and feeling the warmth of her spirit for about twenty minutes, I got back in the car to start making my rounds about the city to collect the money.

After making four stops, the day had stretched into the evening. The sun cast its elongated rays across the asphalt as I gripped the steering wheel, heading to my final spot before returning to the warehouse. My phone buzzed in the center console, and I glanced at the dash, seeing Sienna's name on the screen.

"Hey." I answered her FaceTime call as I rounded the right turn into the driveway.

"Hey, you. I've decided about dinner."

"Yeah? I'm almost done making my rounds, so I'll be back to you soon. What's it gonna be, baby?" I asked as I stepped out of my vehicle.

She grinned at me. "I'm—"

I looked away from the screen, momentarily distracted by the roar of an approaching motorcycle. I saw the flash of a black mask before the rest of her answer was muted by the sound of gunshots ringing through the air.

My entire world tilted as my phone hit the pavement before my body followed. I heard Sienna screaming on the other end of the phone but couldn't move. I couldn't even speak. All I could do was lie there and listen to the sounds around me as the darkness swallowed me whole.

169

there and listen to the sounds around me as the darkness swallowed me whole.

Sienna

My hands trembled as I gripped the phone. The FaceTime call between Ahsan and I had dropped abruptly, but the sound of gunshots still echoed loudly in my ears. Panic surged up my spine, a clear contrast to the simple happiness I'd felt moments ago when talking out my decision about dinner. I'd decided I was going to try and cook for him, but he didn't even get to hear me say the words. *Had I not called about dinner and distracted him, maybe he would've seen it coming.*

I drew a deep breath to steady my racing thoughts before navigating to Amir's social media profile. My fingers typed with urgency, writing out a message that I never imagined I'd have to send. *Amir, it's Sienna. Something bad has happened to Ahsan. Please call me,* I wrote, adding my phone number at the tail of the message before hitting send.

Time slowed to a crawl as I paced the floor, each second feeling like hours until my phone finally buzzed. Amir was on the other line. His voice was a mix of fear and concern. "What the fuck happened to my brother?"

"We were on the phone, and I was talking to him about what to do for dinner when suddenly gunshots rang out of nowhere!"

"Gunshots? Was he hit?"

"I–I don't know. I think so! I kept screaming his name, and he wouldn't answer me, then the call dropped."

"Where was he?"

I yelled out of panic. "I don't know! He left this morning and said he needed to handle some business. That's all I know!"

"Fuck it! Let me check his location." The line went silent for a few minutes before Amir spoke up again. "His location is pinging at Sunrise Valley Hospital. I'm on my way there now. I'll meet you there," he said.

"Okay. I'm on my way!"

THE STERILE HOSPITAL WALLS WERE A MUTED BLUR AS I RUSHED through them, my heart thumping with fear and a pinch of hope that hopefully whatever weapon had formed against him didn't prosper. Ahsan and I couldn't be over before we'd truly begun. Amir was already here, his melanin expression grave as he sat impatiently bouncing his right foot in the waiting room. I inched toward him, and we sat together, silently forming a bond over our shared concern for Ahsan. His fiancée, Brandi, and their cousin, XL, joined us soon after.

When the doctor finally approached, the four of us stood as one, bracing ourselves for the news, come what may. I reached out to hug myself, my hands gripping my shoulders. The doctor explained that Ahsan was stable and his injuries from the shooting were not life-threatening. He had sustained a gunshot wound that resulted in a fractured rib. The medical team acted swiftly to set his rib and manage his pain. A wave of relief washed over me as tears streamed down my face.

I exhaled. "Oh, thank God! Can we go see him?"

"Yes. He can take visitors. We'll keep him overnight for monitoring, and as long as everything checks out with his labs, he'll be good to get discharged in the morning."

"Thank you so much, Doctor!" I thanked him with a genuine smile.

"You're welcome. He's in room two-seventy-three."

The doctor walked away, and Amir shot his eyes over to me. "You really do care about him, don't you?"

I wiped my tears with the back of my hand. I hadn't even realized I'd been crying until then. "Yeah. I do."

He sighed before nodding his head to the side, signaling for us to step off to the side. "Look, I'm sorry I let Jules get in my head the night of my party," he murmured, his voice thick with emotion. "I shouldn't have let a petty ass bet get in between family. We've lost too much time to senseless bullshit that we can't get back."

I nodded, smiling inside because I knew while Ahsan's shooting may have been a terrible event, it was also the thing that would help heal the rift between him and his brother. "I think he'd want you two to come together as a family. You should see him, be there when he wakes up so you can tell him how you feel."

"If you think my brother wants to see my mug over yours after being shot, you buggin'."

I chuckled. "Don't worry; I won't be far behind you."

Amir pulled me into a hug. The past was behind all of us, and ahead was a future where Ahsan and his brother could face anything as long as they did it together.

Ahsan

My hospital room was quiet except for the repeated beeping of the heart monitor stationed next to my bed. There was a knock on the door before it opened. My brother and Sienna stepped inside, their eyes immediately drawn to the fresh bandages wrapped around my torso to keep my ribs set in place. I saw the look of relief in their eyes when they saw me awake and alert.

I caught Sienna's gaze, as she inched toward the bed, and flashed her a weak but reassuring smile to ease her worry. "I promise you it looks worse than it feels," I said lightheartedly, trying to lighten her spirits. "The doctor said the bullet just grazed me. It's gonna take more than that to defeat me. A nigga must got nine lives or something."

"Eight now," she replied, offering a timid but hopeful smile in return.

Amir stood by my bedside with concern etched across his mug. He leaned in closer. "Did you see who the shooter was?" he asked, his voice low and menacing.

My expression turned serious as I shook my head and replied, "Nah, that shit happened too fuckin' fast."

I didn't want to let on that I had a few fragmented memories from the shooting that could be used as clues to unveiling the shooter while Sienna was in the room. But every time I closed my eyes, I recalled the distinct sound of a revving motorcycle engine and the screeching of tires, which suggested that the shooter pulled up on a bike. On top of that, I remembered seeing a flash of a black mask on a nigga with a slim build and locs when I saw the bike before I got hit. I'd been piecing together the puzzle since I woke up in the hospital. I needed to look into my recent conflicts for any signs of betrayal or malice from potential enemies or anyone who might have benefited from wiping my ass off the planet.

"We can't let this shit slide, nigga," my brother argued.

"Baby, could you give us a minute?" I asked Sienna gently. "I need to holla at Amir in private."

"XL is in the hallway," he interjected.

"I'll send him in," Sienna offered, understanding the meaning behind my request.

She nodded and quietly left the room, letting the door shut behind her. XL entered the room soon after. The cheeriness dissolved from my expression once the three of us were alone. I looked at Amir with a hardened intensity that allowed no argument. "I remember the sound of a motorcycle and the flash of a black mask on a nigga with long locs. This shit was planned, y'all," I disclosed, my voice barely above a whisper. "It was an inside job."

XL moved closer, his own expression mirroring mine. "Inside? How do you know?"

"The only people who knew I was making my rounds were—"

"Us, Rico, and Bradley," XL answered, putting the puzzle pieces together just as quickly as I was. "They were at the warehouse with me waiting for you to get back when Bradley said he got a call from you and said you needed him to make a run."

"I never called that nigga. They are the only two who know when we make our weekly rounds to collect the money from the stash houses. I don't know if it was one of them who pulled the trigger, or they paid somebody to do it. Either way, it's safe to say we've got a Judas among us."

"Why the fuck would they bite the hand that feeds them? You think they were looking for a come-up that bad?" Amir asked.

"Maybe. They know I'm transitioning roles and maybe saw it as an opportunity to rank up, cut us out as distro, and go straight to the plug in Mexico. It was bold but stupid as hell. If you gon' shoot me, you better make sure you kill me."

"How much cash did you have on you?" XL inquired.

"About two hundred and fifty thousand before I hit the last house," I answered.

"Fuck!" Amir hissed.

"The money ain't the real problem. We need answers about why they did this."

"We'll figure this shit out, fam," my cousin assured me. "Don't you worry about that. We're in this together, right Amir?"

Amir grunted in agreement. "Hell yeah. Fuck all that other shit. It's in the past. When I find the mothafucka that did this to you, I swear I'll snap his fuckin' neck."

The tension that had once divided us had disappeared in the face of a crisis. "Good, because I need you to do something for me," I told him, my voice firm despite my battered condition. "Find Bradley and Rico. I'm telling you it's someone we know, someone close to our camp."

He wanted me to trust him and see him for the young boss he was. This was his chance to do it.

Amir dipped his chin, a silent vow between us. "I'll find the mothafuckas. I swear."

"What do you need from me?" XL asked, stepping forward.

"I need you to have his back until I'm up and moving around again like I used to. In the meantime, give me daily updates, and keep an eye on Jules for me. After that bullshit she pulled at Amir's party, I don't know what type of shit she's on. Make sure you get her keys from the office and have her turn in her tablet. Then get the IT guy to change all the passwords and the locksmith to have the locks changed around the office," I instructed.

XL nodded before gently dapping me up. "Bet. I got you. Get some rest."

My brother and cousin left the room to start their tasks as I lay back against the stark white hospital pillows. There was a mix of pain and grit in my eyes as I flipped through the rolodex of enemies in my mind. The precision and timing of the attack had led me to believe it was premeditated and not a random act of violence from a stranger.

I had a strong intuition that the shooter was someone from our inner circle, someone we all knew. The road to finding the shooter might have been long, but with Amir and me back on good terms and my family by my side, I knew we would uncover the truth. And when we did, the niggas who'd plotted against me had better pray they had a grandmother still praying for them and God on their side.

Sienna

The next day, I waited outside the hospital entrance, my heart twittering with anticipation. When Ahsan emerged through the automatic sliding doors, my face lit up with uncontrollable delight. I'd found solace in Ahsan's strength, and it was time for me to play the role of the caregiver until he was back to his full self.

"What's got you cheesing so big?" he inquired as I helped him to the car.

"Well, Mr. Businessman, you weren't the only one making big moves over these last few weeks," I explained, my voice bubbling with excitement.

Ahsan looked at me curiously, a smile lifting the edges of his lips despite his pain. "Oh yeah?" he queried, intrigued as he stood by the passenger side door.

I nodded. "I applied to art school *again...* and I got in!" I exclaimed. "The email came in earlier this morning!"

A look of genuine pride washed over Ahsan's handsome face. "Oh shit! That's wassup! I'm so fucking proud of you, Sienna," he said genuinely. "I knew you could do it."

My heart swelled with joy. I couldn't remember the last time I'd heard those words; coming from his lips made it feel even more special.

"Thank you, baby," I replied before kissing his lips.

"I don't know about you, but I want to celebrate," he declared, his spirit alive and well, despite his injuries. "Where you wanna go?"

I belted out a soft chuckle. "Um, no. You're in no condition to celebrate with those ribs. Walking is about the only thing you can do. Besides, all I want is your company and maybe a bottle of champagne."

He kissed my forehead before easing his body into the car. "Anything for you."

BACK AT HIS PLACE, WE SETTLED COMFORTABLY ON THE balcony. With a gentle pop of the cork, I opened a bottle of champagne, watching the bubbles fizz and explode like a volcano. Ahsan raised his glass to me. His eyes locked on mine, his gaze a blend of admiration and pride.

"To you, the dangerously beautiful creature who captured my attention that night at the bar and never let it go. Your dreams are finally taking flight, Sienna. May your artistic talent continue to shine bright like the light you are. I'm proud to be along for the ride on your journey to galleries and greatness. Here's to your success, your strength, and to us—overcoming all life's bullshit together. Cheers, baby."

My eyes glistened with unleashed tears as I listened to his heartfelt toast. I let his kind words wash over me, filling me with belief and pushing me forward as our glasses clinked in unison. It was the first time I felt seen for who I was and the artist I aspired to be.

For a moment, I stood speechless, caught up in my feelings and the moment's intensity. My heart was full, and the words I'd been swallowing down for weeks were once again rising to the surface. The shooting had given me a greater appreciation for life and for Ahsan and what his presence meant to me. Knowing how quickly things could change, I wanted to cherish the moments we had left together. I wanted to be his girl forreal.

I looked up at Ahsan, my eyes meeting his with a mix of courage and vulnerability. "Ahsan, I-I love you. I've been in love with you for a while now, but I've been too afraid to say it. Afraid that it might be too soon or too much, given our situation. But I can't hold it in any longer, especially not after hearing your toast. All bets aside, I wanna be yours, Ahsan."

Ahsan's brown eyes widened, a rush of emotions playing out across his face. He looked at me... and I mean, really looked at me. For a moment, he was silent as if processing the meaning of my words. Then, slowly, a smile started to break through his hardened expression, one that was both tender and filled with reassurance.

"Sienna, hearing you say that, it's like a weight has been lifted off my shoulders. Finding you was like finding a piece of myself I didn't even know I was missing. I love you, too, more than I ever thought was humanly possible with this cold heart of mine."

His words wrapped around me like a gentle embrace as a smile spread across my lips, stretching to my eyes. "Nothing scared me more than the thought of losing you," I confessed. "I was losing my mind on the other end of that phone."

"I know, and I'm sorry you had to witness that, but I'm good, and you don't need to worry about me. All I want you focused on is bussin' ass in art school, all right?" he instructed, his voice steady and sure.

"Okay. I can do that." I agreed.

We inched closer, our palms aligning, a physical sign of our unwavering connection as our two hearts united. Saying those three words to each other was a pivotal moment that marked the start of a new chapter in our lives and our not-so-fake relationship. All the noise and distractions faded away, and all the opposition we'd faced seemed like water under the bridge. We had each other, and in my eyes, that was more than enough.

Ahsan

T*wo weeks later.*

I STIRRED AWAKE, EYES SLOWLY POPPING OPEN TO WITNESS THE first light of dawn peeking through the curtains. I stretched, easing my hand to my left and feeling the soft rhythm of Sienna's breathing in the quiet room. It was my thirty-fifth birthday. A winning smile slowly crept up the corner of my lips as I allowed the significance of the day to wash over me. *Nigga, we made it.*

Although we still hadn't caught up with the shooter, my chest was filled with gratitude. It was a warm, expansive feeling that spread throughout my body, waking me up. I was alive, still above ground, in the land of the living, and in my line of work, that was no small feat. Each breath I took was a testament to my resilience in the game. And as I turned the page to a new chapter in my life, I couldn't help but want to pat myself on the fucking back.

My hand instinctively found my side, fingers tracing the area where the bullet grazed my ribs. My wound was steadily healing. It reminded me of what I'd been through and how fragile life was. I was more than a survivor. Each day, I felt stronger and a little more like my old self again.

Sienna shifted in her sleep. Her presence alone had been a big part of my recovery process. She'd shown a nigga nothing but unwavering love and support. Living together had become a welcomed adjustment. We'd created our own sanctuary and were doing well. I could honestly say I could see myself building a life with her. I'd gone from not trusting women to handing over the key to my heart without her even asking for it.

And then there was the land development project. Slowly but surely, my vision was coming to life, brick by brick. The partnership with the mayor's office was a milestone and my legacy in the making that extended beyond the game.

I was thirty-five and surrounded by the tangible evidence that I was blessed. The adversity I faced only made my wins sweeter. *Big Mama's prayers are still working from the grave.* I promised myself I'd celebrate my life milestone, the love I had, and the endless possibilities that awaited me.

Sienna had orchestrated a full day of curated birthday surprises for me. She knew the importance of the milestone and handled every detail with care. First, she arranged a private art viewing at a local gallery showcasing her work. Next, she planned a surprise picnic in the park, taking a page from my book for our baseball field date. She had all my favorite foods and even hooked up with XL to have him bake me Big Mama's homemade Sock it to Me cake.

Hours later, I stood before the mirror, adjusting the collar of my designer shirt. The fabric was smooth under my fingertips. The fabric was a deep blue. Sienna picked it out, noting something about how the color brought out the warmth in my complexion. I paired it with custom-fitted trousers before slipping into my leather loafers.

"You almost ready, birthday boy?" Sienna asked, sliding her hoop earring into her ear.

I nodded. "Yeah. I'll be done in a second."

I took a moment to draw a deep breath in and slowly exhale to ground myself. It wasn't just any day or any party. It was a celebration of my life and survival. I glanced to my left, feeling the weight of the Rolex on my wrist as the seconds slipped away leading up to the party.

Half an hour later, Sienna and I arrived at the venue. We stepped inside, hand in hand. I looked around, admiring the flashing lights, the DJ spinning at the booth, and the familiar faces of the people I held dear. The music faded, and a chorus of voices sang the first notes of "Happy Birthday," blending in a serenade that made me smile. My heart was filled to the brim with appreciation as I looked around the room at the people in my corner who held me down. I raised my glass and toasted to the love that enveloped me and the many more years to come.

The buzz of my phone broke through the festivities, and an unread text from Amir lit up the screen. I opened it, eyes scanning from left to right. *Need you to ride out with me. ASAP.* There was an uptick in my heartbeat. I knew that tone. His unspoken urgency was a call to action between us.

I turned to Sienna, her brow furrowing in concern as she read my expression. "What is it?"

"I have to go handle some business," I said, my voice steady despite the angst of leaving my celebration.

Her eyes searched mine for answers. "Right now? It's your birthday."

I glanced around the room before my eyes landed back on hers. "I'll be back soon, I promise," I said, praying my words were true. "Stay here and enjoy the party. I won't be too long."

Sienna nodded with understanding before kissing me goodbye.

The soft press of her lips lingered against mine. "Be safe," she whispered, reminding me what was at stake.

"Always."

I stepped out into the night, the music fading behind me as Amir pulled up, and I got inside the car with him.

"I got Bradley," he confirmed. "Caught him in bed with his bitch in a motel three hours away. The nigga had the nerve to be fucking on *our* money."

"That stupid ass mothafucka had the money on him?"

"Yeah, at least some of it, celebrating like he'd won."

"What about Rico?"

He grunted. "Nigga still ain't turn up yet, but he will. I thought you'd want to question Bradley about it before you popped his ass. Happy birthday, nigga."

I scoffed. "Thanks."

THE WAREHOUSE STOOD IN THE STILLNESS OF THE NIGHT. WE exited the car and walked around to the trunk. Amir reached inside the secret compartment and handed me a gun before we stepped inside. The faint smell of sawdust wafted past my nose. The echo of our footsteps was in sync as we walked to the back, passing all the product in shipping containers.

Coming face-to-face with the nigga who'd conspired to take me off the board was a crucial final move before I ultimately transitioned out of the game, one that would set the foundation for Amir's future to keep the Patton name feared in the streets. I walked with purpose, my mind focused on getting answers and the gun at my hip. I approached the pole where Bradley was tied. The harsh light of a hanging bulb illuminated his bloodied face. Before saying anything, I removed my blazer jacket and unbuttoned my dress shirt. I was in my element, the place where I turned dreams into nightmares. I trekked over to him wearing my wife beater and dress trousers.

"Where's Rico and the rest of my fuckin' money?" I questioned, walking over to him with my gun in hand.

"I don't know what you're talking about."

"Fuck this shit!" Amir interjected. "We know it was you and Rico who told the shooter where to go and who to hit. Where the fuck is the rest of the money, nigga? If we find it, we find him."

"Tell us where he's at, and we'll let you go," I told Bradley.

"I can't. I'm not a rat."

"But you are a fucking snake with misplaced loyalty," I growled, gripping the gun tighter and smacking him across the face with it.

He groaned in pain as his head hung low. "Ahhh shit!"

"Where the fuck is Rico at? That nigga left you hanging out to dry! He should be here, too, receiving the consequences for his actions witchu. Tell me where he is while you still have a choice!" I hissed.

"Only choice I got is death, and I ain't afraid to die, nigga!" Bradley spat, blood dripping from his face.

I grunted. I hated having to take accountability for my poor judgment of character. It was my fault for expecting too much from niggas and giving them the benefit of the doubt. If their disloyalty taught me anything, it was that loyalty was earned, and so was betrayal. Everybody wasn't meant to go to the next level with me.

"Good, because if you thought you could try to take my life, steal from me, and I'd let you walk away, you were sadly mistaken. If you play, you lay, bitch nigga."

I pulled the trigger twice, ending his life with ease and letting his death be a lesson of what would happen if *anyone* ever tried to go against me again.

"Get the hydrofluoric acid from the back. Let's get this shit cleaned up," I instructed, ready to dissolve his body.

THE COOL NIGHT AIR BRUSHED AGAINST MY FACE AS I rebuttoned my shirt to cover the blood splatter on my wife beater. I slid my jacket back over my shoulders before leaving the warehouse. A sense of accomplishment settled in my bones as I listened to the quiet hum of the bustling city in the distance. The night sky was clear, the stars above the only witnesses to the murder within the warehouse's walls.

"So, how does it feel to be thirty-five, nigga?" Amir asked as we got back into his car and returned to my party.

I paused, a soft smile spreading across my face. "Grateful," I replied, summing up my feelings with one word. I clapped my right hand on Amir's shoulder, a sincere gesture. "And I owe a lot of that to you, my boy. Your loyalty means a lot to me."

A moment of silence passed between us before my expression softened, a twinge of guilt in my gaze. "Yo, listen. I need to apologize for rigging that bet," I confessed, my gaze dropping to my lap. "It was out of love. I just wanted to protect you."

Amir nodded, understanding the weight of my words. "Say less, nigga. I get it. I understood your logic once I got out of my feelings about everything. You're right. I do have a lot to lose now."

"And I want you to know, Sienna and I... we're the real deal now. I love her."

His brows heightened. "What? She got you saying the L-word all loud and proud?"

"Shut up. But tell me, how did you know you were ready to propose to Brandi? How did you see through all y'all bullshit and know she was the one?" I asked, voice tinged with apprehension.

Amir chuckled, a lightness in his tone. "It wasn't one thing, you know? I just woke up one day, had a ring on my mind, and went to the jeweler. Why? You thinking about walking down that aisle soon too?"

"Not today, but maybe one day soon. I know we haven't been together long, but whenever I make that next move, I know I want it to be with her."

"That's wassup, nigga. I'm happy for you."

"Thanks, and speaking of next moves, I think this goes without saying, but I officially want you to take over. It's time to focus on my land development project full time, just as I planned. You ready to step up to the plate?"

Amir's eyes widened, a mix of surprise and honor washing over his stern expression. "You forreal? Officially?"

"Yeah, officially," I confirmed with a nod. "You've earned it, and I trust you more than anybody else with this."

"Thank you, Ahsan. I won't let you down, nigga," he said, dapping me up.

I glanced out the window, feeling a surge of pride. Handing the business to Amir was more than a new chapter; it was proof of our unbreakable bond as brothers.

I returned to the party, and Sienna greeted me with the type of smile that lit up the entire room. I let the events of the warehouse fade into the back of my mind, but the statement I'd left lingered, a silent lesson on what would come if anyone crossed me or my family again.

"There you are." Sienna greeted me, her voice blending joy and relief. "I thought you'd miss out on your entire party. But don't worry, I saved you a corner piece of birthday cake with extra frosting."

I smirked. "Thank you. Just how I like it."

She led me to the table where the remains of my birthday cake awaited. As promised, she'd set a slice aside just for me, untouched and perfect.

"Make a wish so we can go home, and I'll let you eat that cake off my cake," she urged, her eyes dazzling with mischief.

I nodded, feeling the urgency behind her words. With a deep breath, I closed my eyes and made a silent wish. Then, with a grin, I tasted a bite of the cake and then kissed her. The sweetness of the cake and Sienna's lips was a perfect end to my day.

Sienna

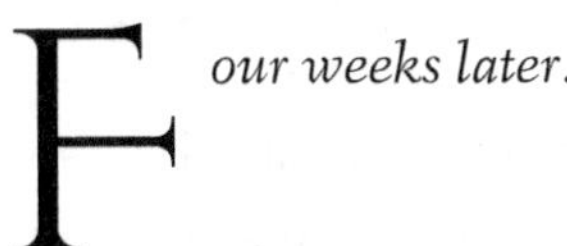

our weeks later.

THE WEEKEND SUN GLOWED OVER THE CITY AS I ADDED THE final strokes to my canvas. I stood back from my latest work. The balcony of Ahsan's apartment had become my sanctuary, the place where my creativity flowed freely. My journey back to art school lay ahead, only a few days away before classes started. My mind was a jumble of anticipation and excitement.

Ahsan stepped out onto the balcony, interrupting my daze. He smiled brightly. His ribs were fully healed, no longer a reminder of the pain and betrayal he'd endured.

"Hey, you," he said softly, leaning against the doorframe. "How's it going?"

"Just finished. All that's left to do is put my signature on it," I replied.

"Got a name for this one?"

"I don't know yet. How about you name it?"

"Me?"

I giggled. "Yeah, you. What comes to mind when you look at it?"

Ahsan stared at it for a moment, his eyes reflecting the colors of my painting. He inched closer, taking in the swirls of yellow and bursts of orange that danced across my canvas. "It's dope," he said honestly.

I bit my lip, watching him study my painting as the colors spoke to him. The longer I watched him, the more turned-on I became. I walked up to him and wrapped my arms around his waist.

"How about 'Echoes of Dreams'?" he suggested.

"Echoes of Dreams," I repeated, tasting the words as they bounced off my tongue. A smile spread across my face. "I think that's perfect. Thank you."

"It's you that I've been meaning to thank."

My brows creased. "Me? For what?"

"For being there for me when I was at my lowest. I know it wasn't a serious gunshot wound, but you stayed by my side. You showed me you're not here for the good times or the money. You're here for a nigga."

"Ahsan, I—"

He held up a hand with a playful yet serious look in his eyes. "Pack a bag," he announced.

"We're going to Miami for the weekend. Just you and me." His surprise announcement hung in the air, a spontaneous yet romantic gesture.

The paintbrush fell from my fingers, hitting the ground as I hooked my paint-splattered arms around him. "Oh my God! Are you serious?" I asked, my excitement barely contained.

"Yeah. Our flight leaves in four hours. We can either go into the bedroom and get packed, or we can get an early start on our romantic getaway with a little horizontal horseplay and buy all new clothes when we get there. It's up to you," he suggested before kissing my neck gently.

A whirlwind of emotions swept through me as my heartbeat quickened with excitement. A fluttering sensation of butterflies danced up from the pit of my stomach to my chest. Miami was a dream. Going back to my roots was what I needed to recenter my mind and ground myself before starting school. My mind raced with pictures of sandy beaches, the roaring waves, and the two of us alone and disconnected from the real world, if only for seventy-two hours.

Gratitude washed over me. I'd never been catered to by a man like that before. It was a clear reminder of Ahsan's thoughtfulness. Our getaway was more than a weekend escape; it was a celebration of our love for each other and the life we were building together.

Two and a half weeks later.

I wheeled my grocery cart down the aisle while repeating my list in my mind—*ice cream, almond milk, grapes, and... a pregnancy test*. My heart fluttered at the thought. I was a ball of nerves and excitement. I'd only been back in school for a few weeks and felt slightly off after returning from Miami. I didn't know if it was the nerves of being back in school full time or something else.

The fluorescent grocery store lights hung over me as I turned the corner onto the aisle with the frozen food lockers. My pace instantly slowed. There he was, Demario. His presence was like a dark rain cloud in my otherwise sunny sky. I couldn't avoid him; our paths were destined to cross between the ice cream and frozen waffles.

He approached me, his long locs twisted in a bun on top of his head and a smirk playing on his lips. "Are congratulations in order?" he queried, his eyes darting down to the pregnancy test in my cart.

His question taunted me as I straightened my posture, keeping my voice steady. "That's none of your business."

"You'll always be my business, baby girl, even when you *think* you're with another nigga."

"I don't think—I know I'm in a relationship, and I'm happy! I don't want anything to do with your black ass anymore," I declared, my words slicing through the tension.

His expression hardened, his smirk replaced by a scowl. "I just gave up the last five fucking years of my freedom for you," he spat, his tone menacing. "You owe me that time back."

A cold chill raced down my spine as his words echoed in my ears. I immediately felt threatened as dark thoughts ran through my mind. It became clear that I would have to tell Ahsan about my run-in with Demario. He needed to know in case Demario's unhinged ass became a potential threat to the peaceful life we were building together.

I quickly wheeled away, speeding past him. I couldn't believe he'd claimed to have sacrificed his life for me when he was the reason his life had taken a dark turn marked by years in prison. His return was nothing but a sense of entitlement and a misplaced desire to reclaim whatever fragments of our relationship he believed he lost. He was trying to tie me to a debt I knew I didn't owe. I darted out of the store. Our encounter was a chilling realization that the past could resurface at any given moment.

Ahsan

The door to the apartment closed with a soft click behind Sienna. She leaned against it while drawing in a deep breath, trying to shake off whatever she'd encountered on the other side of that door. I immediately noticed the distress in her stiffened posture.

"What's wrong?" I questioned, voice laced with concern as I rose from the couch to meet her.

She hesitated, her words caught in her throat. "I was at the grocery store when I ran into my ex," she stated, the story quickly spilling off her tongue. "He... he made some threats about how I owed him for the time he spent locked up."

My jaw tightened, and a protective fire ignited in my eyes. "Hold up, that nigga threatened you? What the fuck did he say exactly? And what does he look like? You got a picture?"

Sienna unlocked her phone, tapping against the screen and scrolling before she flipped it my way. The nigga looked like a squid with dreads, and I would've been more than happy to turn his locs into spaghetti just like I did the nigga from the hotel party that hurt

Sienna. If he was looking for smoke behind Sienna, I wasn't the nigga to play with.

I pulled her into my arms. "Don't worry, baby. I'll have my brother look into it. I promise you we'll take care of it. I won't let a piece of your past disrupt what we've built."

My words weren't just reassurance but my solemn vow that I would always stand on business, fight for her, and ensure our future together was as peaceful as possible.

My brain moved at a million miles a minute, considering all the ways to address the situation with Sienna's bitch ass ex, including personal precautions to keep her safe. In my heart, I knew I had to ensure her safety and peace of mind above all else. But the idea that someone from her past had resurfaced to cause her distress had me ready to revert to my old ways and pull him apart limb by fucking limb.

THE NIGHT HAD SETTLED IN WHEN MY SCREEN LIT UP WITH A text from Jules. I hadn't heard from her since I fired her jealous ass.

Jules: *Isn't it funny how secrets never stay buried? Some of your foundations might not be as solid as you think. Sleep well, boss man.*

I read the message repeatedly, trying to decipher the meaning behind her cryptic words, but it only heightened my alarm. Her words were vague enough to keep her intentions unclear yet suggestive enough to send a ripple of unease through me. She was playing games on my phone and hinting at disrupting my peace. It wasn't just about business; this shit was personal and a direct blow to the safety and stability I'd spent years building around me.

Without hesitation, I dialed XL's number. The phone rang three times, slicing through the silence until I heard his familiar voice. "Wassup?"

"We've got a situation," I confirmed, my words sharp with urgency.

"What's good?"

"I just got some cryptic ass message from Jules. We need to figure out what our next move is. You had no problems when you had her drop off her equipment, right?"

"Nah. Shit has been quiet. I put a tail on her like you asked me for that first month, but she didn't move out of the ordinary."

"Well, I think she's about to make one soon if she hasn't already."

"Say less. I'll call Amir. Let's meet at the warehouse in an hour. We'll decide how to handle this. We're not going to let mothafuckas shake us up again."

I hung up, a plan formulating in my mind. I knew the three of us together would find a solution. The night might have brought some unexpected threats, but I refused to let them knock me off my square.

I walked down the hallway to the bedroom to find Sienna and told her I would meet with XL and Amir. "You need anything while I'm out?"

"Can you pick up a pregnancy test?"

I froze. Her question hung in the air, and the weight of possibility hung over me. The thought of us possibly starting a family so soon had never crossed my mind. "A pregnancy test?" I repeated, my voice a blend of surprise and unease.

She nodded with a nervous energy about her. "I'm sorry for springing it on you like this. I was supposed to grab one at the store, but after seeing Demario, I left without buying a damn thing."

"Hold up. You're pregnant, Sienna?"

"I'm not sure, but I'm almost a week late," she admitted, watching my reaction closely.

I stood frozen for a few more seconds, letting the weight of her words settle over me. Then, a smile began to spread across my lips slowly. My initial shock transitioned into growing excitement. The idea of becoming a father, something I never had, ignited a warmth inside me.

"Okay, baby. I'll pick one up. No matter what it says, I got you."

I gave her a reassuring kiss before leaving the apartment. My mind raced with thoughts of our impending future. As I drove to meet up with my cousin and brother, the night started to feel a little brighter. Life was full of surprises, and I was ready to embrace whatever was next.

———

After meeting with Amir and XL to get them up to speed on the situation with Sienna's ex and Jules, I walked through the automatic doors of the local pharmacy. I headed straight for the aisle, which I had never thought I'd visit so soon. My eyes scanned the shelves filled with different brands of pregnancy tests. My hand hovered from left to right before picking up a random box. I paid for it and made my way back home.

When I arrived, I found Sienna sitting anxiously on the couch. I handed her the plastic bag with the box inside, our fingers gently touching. "I'll be right back," she announced before disappearing down the hall and into the bathroom. I followed closely behind her, waiting outside the door until she joined me. "Can you set your timer for five minutes?" she asked.

I nodded.

Tick. Tock. Each second seemed to stretch on longer than the last. When the alarm finally chimed, I looked at her. "You ready?"

Sienna quickly shook her head. "I can't look," she said, her voice layered with nerves. "Please, can you do it?"

"Yeah. I got you."

My heart raced as I pushed the bathroom door open. The plastic stick lay on the counter. I took a deep breath and looked down at the test with a single line in the results window. I picked up the instructions to understand the results. *Negative.* I let out a breath I didn't realize I'd been holding and walked back into the bedroom.

Sienna looked up at me with a question in her eyes. "Well?"

I sat down beside her on the bed and took her hand. "It's negative," I said gently.

A complex wave of emotions washed over me. Relief was the first to surface as the immediate weight of fatherhood lifted from my shoulders. We still had dreams and plans that having a baby might have complicated. But beneath my relief was a pang of disappointment as thoughts of what could have been flooded my mind. Sienna and I had faced the possibility of becoming parents together, if only for a few hours, and having to face the reality that we weren't felt like a small blow. The negative result didn't change my feelings for her, though. If anything, it deepened our relationship by facing the possibility of *'what if'* together.

She leaned into me, finding comfort in my arms. "We have time," she whispered.

I nodded. "We do."

Epilogue

S ienna

Two weeks had passed since the night the pregnancy test turned up negative. Sometimes, in the quiet moments of my day, I found my thoughts pining over the what-ifs and maybes. I wasn't sad, not really. Yet, a silent longing flickered inside me from time to time.

I knew in my heart that when the time was right, everything would unfold as it was meant to. Until then, I would continue to pour my feelings into my blank canvases.

My vibrating phone came as a gentle interruption to my afternoon. I saw the Gallery at Forestbrook across the screen, and my heart skipped a beat.

"Hello?" I answered on the second ring.

"Hi, Sienna. It's Nia, the curator from the Gallery at Forestbrook. We have an interested buyer for your work, and they're eager to meet the artist behind the masterpiece. Can you come in for a quick meet and greet?"

My heart somersaulted in my chest. "Yes! Of course! I'll be right there," I replied, filled with delight.

I ARRIVED AT THE GALLERY HALF AN HOUR LATER, MY STEPS quick. But as I stepped inside, the sight that greeted my eyes was nothing like what I expected. A trail of crimson red rose petals and tealight candles carpeted the floor, stretching from the entrance throughout the gallery. My heart raced as my eyes curiously followed the path. Ahsan stood at the end of the rose trail surrounded by art. His smile was bright, and his brown orbs dazzled with desire.

The gallery was empty, reserved just for us. That was when I realized I'd been lured here under false pretenses. He'd bought out the space for the evening and transformed it into a private romantic oasis. The shadows of the flickering flames seemed to move in sync with the soft R&B music playing throughout the space. The lyrics to Musiq Soulchild's "Love" whispered through the space, speaking directly to my feelings for him. He'd curated every enchanting detail.

Tears welled in my eyes, a crashing wave of joy overwhelming me. "Oh my God, baby. What is all this?" I asked, still shocked.

"I wanted to create the perfect setting for you," Ahsan replied, stepping forward to take my hands in his. "Because you are my muse, my baby, and my only love." Ahsan dropped to one knee, surrounded by the roses and flickering candlelight. "Sienna Bennett, there are some things that can't be explained with words. But the way you make me feel isn't one of them. Over these past few months, I've learned a lot about you and myself. For instance, I know you needed somebody with self-control, and I needed somebody who could bring me peace. You needed somebody who would go the extra mile for you, and I needed a woman who'd pray for me like Big Mama used to. Your presence has brought me a level of peace I never knew existed, and I never want to let you go. Will you marry me?" he asked, his voice assured.

Time seemed to stand still. It was a fairy tale suspended in utter perfection and a memory forever etched in my mind. The outside world faded away until nothing was left but Ahsan and me. His words were more than a proposal. They were a lasting dedication of his heart to mine.

"Yes," I whispered as tears streamed down my face. "Yes, I'll marry you, baby!" I squealed.

THE END

Afterword

A note from K.L. Hall.

Reader,

Thank you for reading *Make Mine a Gangsta: The Patton Brothers Book One*. If you've made it this far, I hope you'll consider telling me what you thought about the book in the form of a **five-star review and/or rating**. Don't hesitate to let me know what you'd like to see from me next! I thoroughly enjoy reading your thoughts and hearing from you as well! I'm always striving to attract new readers and retain current ones, and reviews are one of the easiest ways to attract readers. If you loved the book, tell a friend, and most importantly, let me know!

All my love,
K.L. Hall

About the Author

K.L. Hall is a national bestselling and award-winning author. As a serial storyteller, Hall has penned over three dozen titles in various genres—including African American urban fiction and romance, paranormal, children's books (as Kimberley M.), and non-fiction. Her fictional stories straddle the intersection of classic Urban and spell-binding Romance.

Highly Acclaimed Titles:
In the Arms of a Savage: (Peaked at #1 in Women's Fiction)
The Potomac Falls Series (Peaked at #1 and #2 in African American Erotica)

Sign up for my mailing list to stay updated with new releases, giveaways, sneak peeks, and more! Click this link: https://bit.ly/38RMpV5

Connect with me on social media:
Facebook: https://www.facebook.com/authorklhall
Twitter: https://twitter.com/authorklhall
Instagram: https://www.instagram.com/officialklhall/
Website: https://www.authorklhall.com

Other novels by K.L. Hall:
Diary of a Hood Princess 1-3
Rise of a Street King: The Justice Silva Story (*Spin-Off to the Diary of a Hood Princess series*)

Broken Condoms and Promises 1-3

In the Arms of a Savage 1-3

Built for a Savage: Blaze and Camille's Love Story (*Spin-Off to the In the Arms of a Savage Series*)

A Ruthle$$ Love Story 1-3

Fallin' for the Alpha of the Streets 1-2

The Most Savage of Them All: The Wolfe Calloway Story (*Prequel to the In the Arms of a Savage Series*)

When a Gangsta Loves a Good Girl

Caught Between My Husband and a Hustler

The Illest Taboo 1-2

To the Only Thug I'll Ever Love

A Lover's Heist: Chief and Gianna's Love Story

A Lover's Heist II: Rome and Lira's Love Story

A Lover's Heist III: Baby and Skai's Love Story

Crushed Velvet & Cashmere

Crushed Velvet & Cashmere 2

Entanglements

Never Had a Bad Boy Love Me So Good

Good Girls Always Got a Thing for the Thugs

Professor Zaddy: A Potomac Falls Novel

Bound in the Arms of a Thug: Chop & Kendyl's Love Story

Make Mine a Gangsta: The Patton Brothers Book One

Short Reads + Novellas:

Bi-Curious: An Erotic Tale

Bi-Curious 2: Tastes Like Candy

A Savage Calloway Christmas (*Christmas novella to the In the Arms of a Savage Series*)

Lovin' the Alpha of the Streets: A Valentine's Day Novella (*Valentine's Day novella to the Fallin' for the Alpha of the Streets Series*)

Awakened: A Paranormal Romance

As Long as You Stay Down

Solace in Seven

Solace II: The Final Cut

Something Bleu

Something Borrowed

Something New

The Knight Before Christmas: A Potomac Falls Short

I'll Be Home for Christmas: A Potomac Falls Short Book II

Triggered: A Potomac Falls Novella

Wasted Off You: A Friends to Lovers Novella

Because You Don't Know My Name: A Potomac Falls Novella

Will You Say My Name: A Potomac Falls Novella Book Two

Remember My Name: A Potomac Falls Novella Book Three

Every Thug Needs a Lady: A Lady and the Tramp Retelling

Ten Things I Hate About Lovin' You: An Enemies to Lovers Novella

In Exchange: An Urban Thriller

T.A.N.: An Erotic Novella

Children's Books:

Princess for Hire

Princess Twinkle Toes & the Missing Magic Sneakers

Little One, Change the World

Adjust Your Crown: A Self-Love Coloring Book for Children of Color

Non-Fiction:

Authors are a Business: The Booked & Busy Course Mini Book